THE LEGENDARY BOYS
FROM ACROSS THE RIVER
WHO HAVE BECOME

The Boys of '54

THE LEGENDARY BOYS
FROM ACROSS THE RIVER
WHO HAVE BECOME

The Boys of '54

A MYTH

E. Calvin Golumbic

The Legendary Boys From Across The River Who Have Become The Boys of '54, A Myth

First Edition
First Printing

ISBN: 979-8-218-71980-7

Printed in United States of America

Publishing Assistance provided by:
Heimat Publishing, Crystal Heidel

THE LEGENDARY BOYS
FROM ACROSS THE RIVER
WHO HAVE BECOME

The Boys of '54

IN HONOR
OF
MY CLASSMATES.

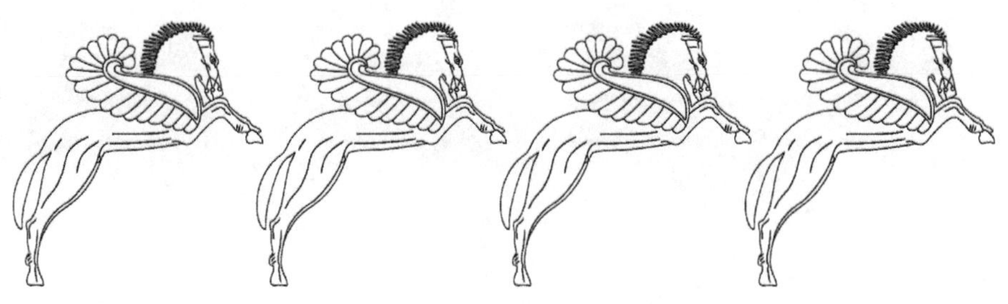

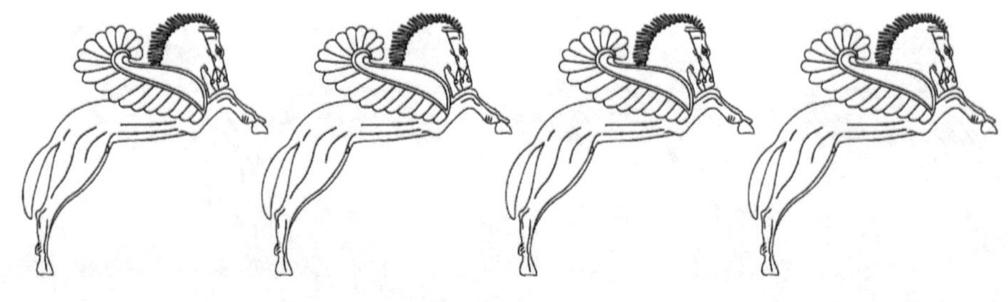

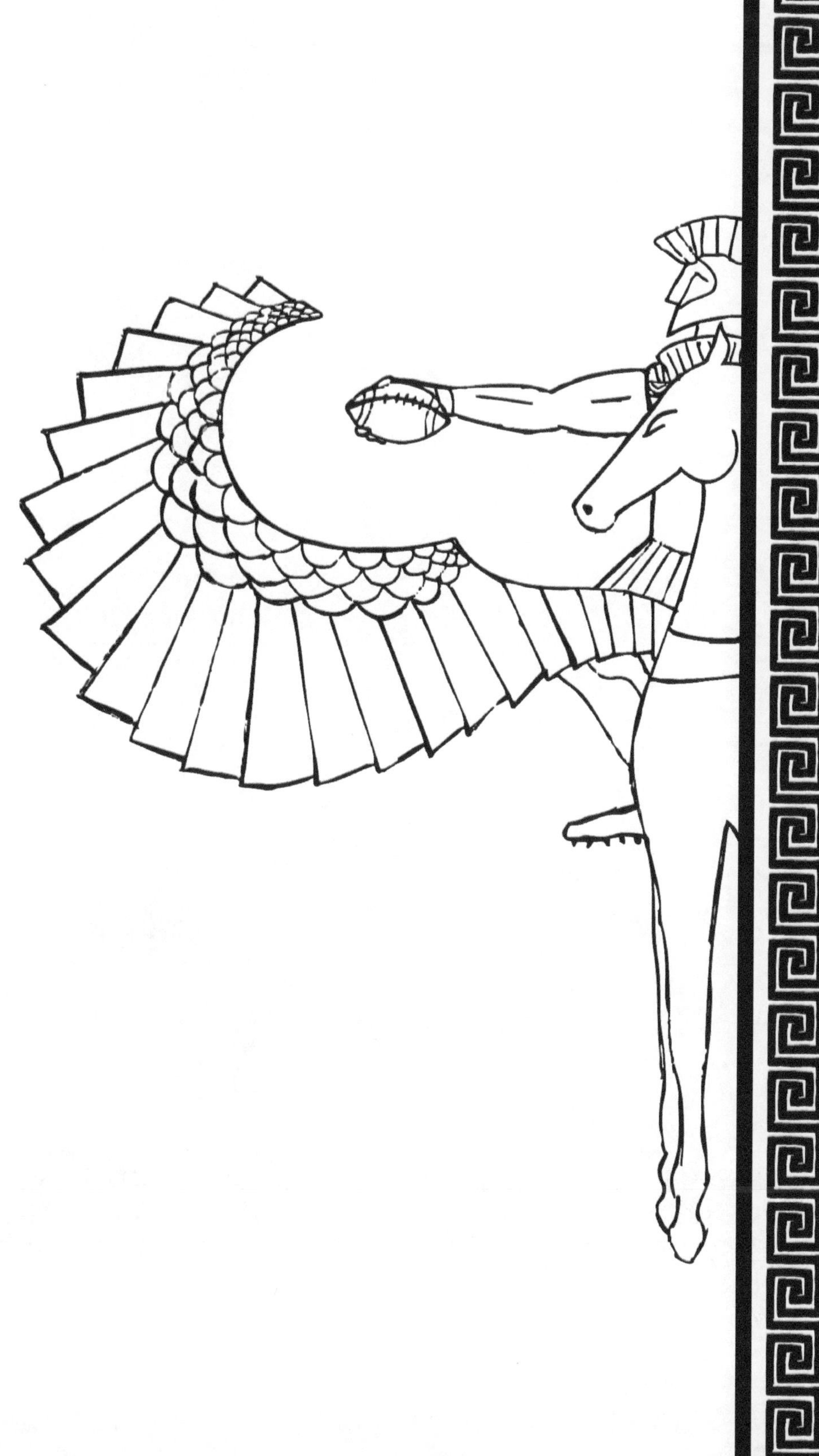

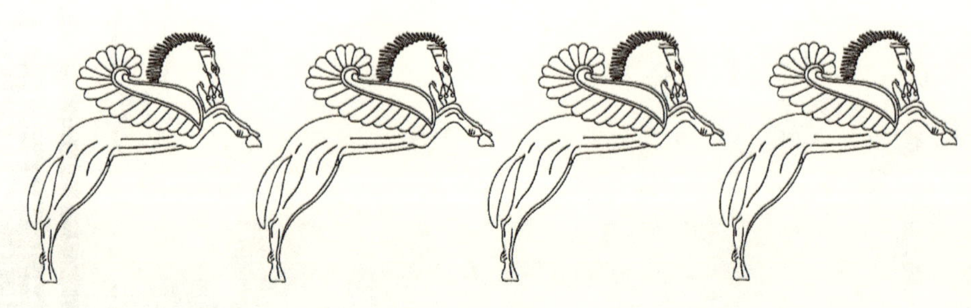

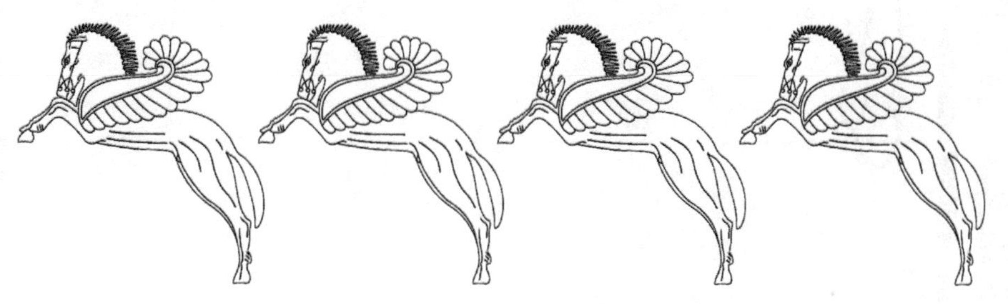

TABLE OF CONTENTS

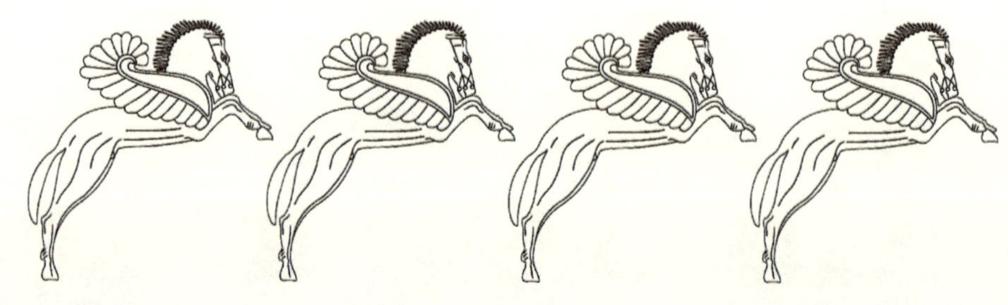

FOREWORD

SOME MAY SAY that this is a football story. Others may say that it is a high school football story. Others may say that it is a story about a high school football team. Others may say that it is a story about a high school football team from a small town. Others may say that it is a story about a high school football team from a small town in the Appalachian Mountains. Others may say that it is a story about a high school football team from a small town in the Appalachian Mountains in the early 1950s. Others may say that it is a story about a high school football team from a small town in the Appalachian Mountains that finished the season unbeaten and untied in the early 1950s. Others may say that it is a story about a high school football team from a small town in the Appalachian Mountains that finished the season undefeated and untied by defeating a number football teams from high schools that were much larger than their own in the early 1950s. And others may say that it is a story about a high school football team from a small town in the Appalachian Mountains that became legendary by finishing the season undefeated and untied by defeating a number of football teams from high schools that were much larger than their own in the early 1950s. But whatever else that may be said about that football team, everyone who has grown up in that mountainous region agrees that the legend is really about "The Boys," who decided to cross the West Branch of the Susquehanna River, in order to play football for the perennially pathetic "Bobcats" of Lock Haven High School in 1954.

Their unbelievable and indescribable play on a high school gridiron that season against any kind of a football team from any kind of a high school, large or small, was, ostensively, why they ended that season unbeaten and untied. But that story, which is their story, that has become this story, is about more than that seasonal outcome on those football fields; it is about something that happened on those fields, each week, which became legendary at the time, not to mention the subject of folklore, thereafter, about "The Boys From Across The River," who have, eventually, become, with time, discussion and disbelief, the, mythical, "Boys of '54."

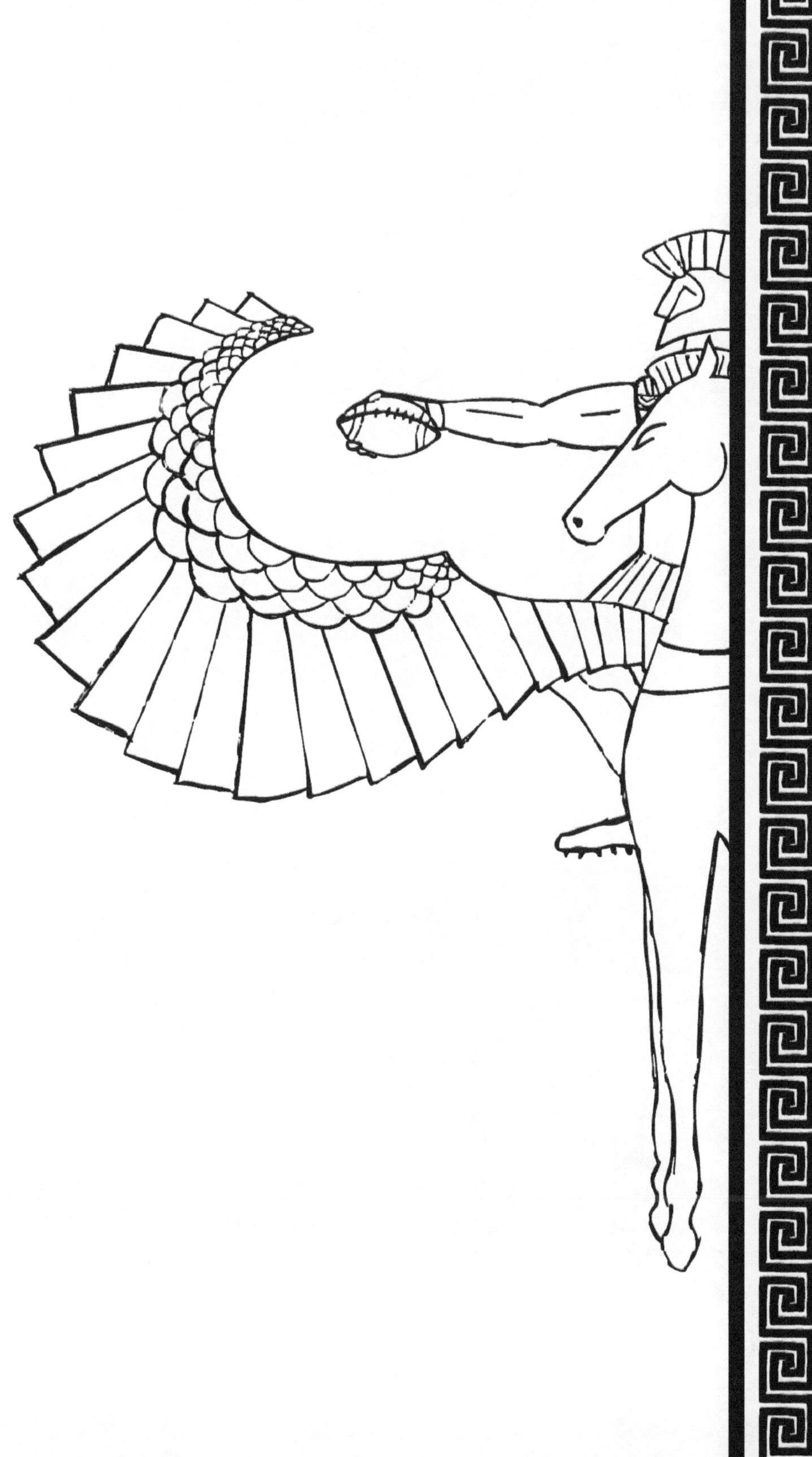

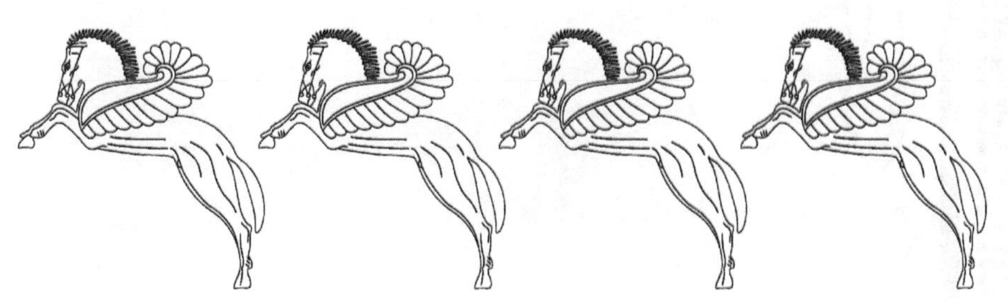

INTRODUCTION

THE TRANSFER OF A NUMBER OF FOOTBALL PLAYERS TO THE LOCK HAVEN HIGH SCHOOL, INCLUDING THOSE WHO CROSSED THE WEST BRANCH OF THE SUSQUEHANNA RIVER, IN ORDER TO PLAY FOR THE "PURPLE AND WHITE," A SCHOLASTIC FOOTBALL TEAM OTHERWISE KNOWN AS THE "BOBCATS," WAS, ACCORDING TO THE FOLKLORE THAT HAD ARISEN IN THAT AREA, THE REASON WHY THE TEAM WAS UNBEATEN AND UNTIED THAT SEASON.

NO ONE KNOWS, anymore, why they came, but we still know most of their names, which are John Englert, Dave Johnson, Wayne Englert, Jack Roller, Tom Toner, Bill Goodman and Lester "Huck" Derr; too much time has passed in the seventy year interval, and, of course, most of them have died, years ago. Some say that it was because they wanted to play for a larger high school, like the Lock Haven High School; others say that it was because Charles "Chub" Schiavo was already there, one of the most valuable players on the "Little League Team" that defeated Pensacola, Florida, six to five, to win the "Little League World Series," a few years ago, in Williamsport, Pennsylvania.

Well, it is certainly true that, subsequent thereto, baseball had given way to the game of football, especially during the fall season of that year, and that "Chub" had decided to exchange his baseball paraphernalia for a pair of cleats and a football helmet, far more appropriate for gridiron glory, especially on a high school football field. And it is certainly true that there was only one "Chub" Schiavo in that world, or, for that matter, any other world at the time, whether we are talking about a baseball diamond, a basketball court or a football field, and "The Boys" certainly knew that!

Notwithstanding that notable fact, or, rather, those notable facts, and "Chub" Schiavo was that "notable," in almost any athletic arena, I prefer to believe that most of them came because Dave Johnson wanted them to come. Although some have said, in that regard, that John Englert may have been a better athlete, which may have actually been true, because of his kicking ability, if nothing else, but it was certainly a very close question. And aside from the answer to such a difficult and historic question, Dave was always their acknowledged leader, especially during the season, playing at the quarterback position, which did not change, even after the season had ended.

Why they came, however, is really immaterial, at least for purposes of this story, because the fact that they did really changed everything, even before the season had actually begun. It certainly explained why Bill Karch, subsequently, decided to leave the Bald Eagle Nittany High School "Panthers," in order to come down to play for the Lock Haven High School "Bobcats." And Bill's subsequent prowess, as a lineman for the "Purple and White," was so remarkable that he was nicknamed, "Midnight," by the rest of the team, because it was lights-out, as it was said, for anyone facing him on the line of scrimmage!

Aware, by now, of what had just transpired over the summer, upriver that is, in the town of Lock Haven, with the arrival of "Chub" Schiavo and Bill Karch, Jack Houser decided to transfer from the "Millionaires" of Williamsport High School, where he had been an outstanding lineman for the "Cherry and White," and, instead, play the following season for the "Purple and White" of Lock Haven High School. Jack's subsequent play that season, at the center position, was as impressive as his size, which was so large that it resulted in a descriptive appellation, on and off the field, as the "Moose."

Even as big as the "Moose" was, however, and he was that big, he was not the largest player on that football team. No, that distinction belonged to Jan Bennett, all six foot seven inches of him, even without his cleats and helmet, I may gratuitously add. Given that size and his athletic ability, which may have even exceeded his size, metaphorically, that is, he was also, not surprisingly, an "All State" basketball player for the "Purple and White," in the previous year, who decided to leave the "hardwood," temporarily, of course, because of the oncoming football season, and what it promised to become, in light of what had already geographically and demographically transpired over the course of that summer. Interestingly enough, he subsequently acquired the "name-de-guerre" of "Bender," on and off the gridiron, likely for no other reason than he became one of the greatest left ends on a high school football team that season in the State of Pennsylvania, if not in the Nation, itself.

With an accumulation of that kind of football talent, at least on the practice field, Tom Toner, one of the finest lineman to ever come out of the sleepy village of Farrrandsville, which was no more than a gap in those mountains, decided to cross the West Branch of the Susquehanna River, too, in order to join the rest of "The Boys," that summer, on the practice fields of J. Arlington Painter Stadium. Interestingly enough, by the end of that season, he had become known, largely in the locker room, as the "Tom Cat," for his prowess both on and off the football fields!

Along with a number of other young men who were from town, such as Dave Smith, Wes Maggs, Ken Miller and Bob Crissman, they formed the nucleus of a team that joined Coach Nelson ("Nels") Hoffman, on those practice fields, whom "The Boys" called "Nails," away from those fields, of course, because of his demanding manner on the fields. Likely because of that fact, or those demands, which continued throughout that summer and extended on into the early fall, prior to the season, itself, the linemen became more than proficient in their offensive and defensive schemes, while the backfield became just as adept at running, in a manner of speaking, the old, "single wing" formation. It was an offense that the Coach decided to employ that season, rather than one of the more currently popular formations, because of the size and speed of his extraordinarily talented running backs.

Visually confirming some of those descriptive facts is a photograph of that backfield, set forth below, with play-calling Dave Johnson at quarterback, line-smashing Bill Goodman at left halfback, fleet-footed "Chub" Schiavo at right halfback, and versatile John Englert at fullback, where he was actually a triple threat, not only as a powerful running back, but as a kicking and passing specialist, as well.

Backfield—Chub Schiavo, Bill Goodman, Dave Johnson, John Englert.

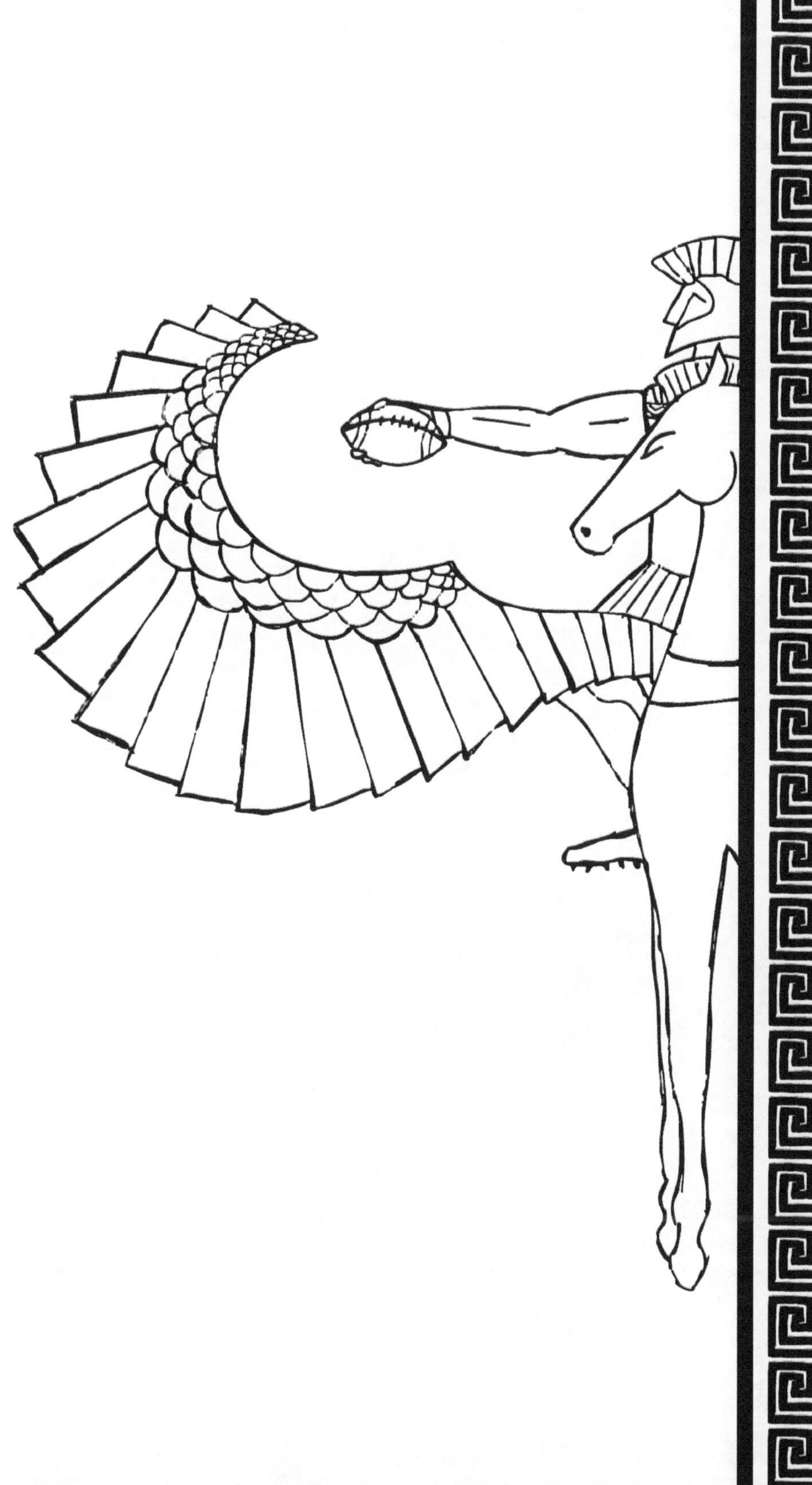

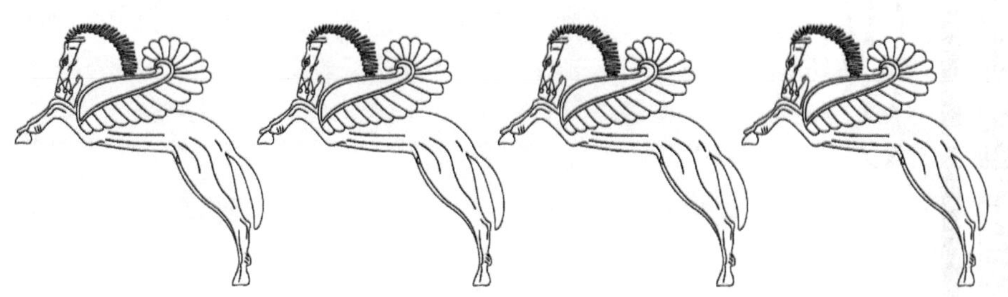

THE FIRST GAME

"THE BOYS" WHO CROSSED THE WEST BRANCH OF THE SUSQUEHANNA RIVER, IN ORDER TO PLAY FOOTBALL FOR THE LOCK HAVEN HIGH SCHOOL "BOBCATS," IN CLINTON COUNTY, PREVAILED, UNEXPECTEDLY, IN THEIR VERY FIRST GAME OF THE SEASON, AGAINST AN OVERLY CONFIDENT TEAM OF "LITTLE LIONS" FROM THE STATE COLLEGE HIGH SCHOOL IN, NEARBY, CENTRE COUNTY, BY THE INEXPLICABLE SCORE OF "TWENTY TO NOTHING," EVEN THOUGH THAT HIGH SCHOOL WAS MUCH LARGER THAN THEIR OWN, AND, FOR THAT MATTER, IT WAS LOCATED IN A MUCH LARGER BOROUGH OF STATE COLLEGE AND IN THE FAR MORE AFFLUENT COMMUNITY OF CENTRE COUNTY.

Finished with their weekly practice, if not the daily demands of their Coach, by the second week of September, "The Boys From Across The River," as the team became subsequently known, suited-up and traveled, southwestwardly, by a dilapidated, yellow school bus, for approximately twenty six miles, up Route 64, to confront the "Little Lions" of State College High School in the Borough of State College, which was located in Centre County, Pennsylvania.

It had not been a very pleasant trip, let alone an enjoyable experience, for the members of a football team from Lock Haven High School, in, nearby, Clinton County, not for a number of years. That was largely due to the demographics in the rapidly developing Borough of State College and, correspondingly, to its rapidly expanding High School, located therein, both of which had begun to dwarf the smaller town of Lock Haven, and, correspondingly, its much smaller high school, both of which were located in a, nearby, rural and far less affluent Clinton County. And that demographic and economic disadvantage, as well as an associated competitive one, had continued to widen, unfairly, each year on the football field!

Indeed, because of those elevated demographics, the High School in State College had recently joined a football conference of much larger public high schools, including the one in the City of Altoona and the one in the City of Johnstown, among a number of others with, similarly, impressive demographics and, correspondingly, more formidable football programs, known as the Western Conference. But it continued to play a few smaller high schools with, correspondingly, smaller football programs, like the ones in Lock Haven and Bellefonte, probably more out of proximity

than anything else, with an associated history of winning results against both of those noncompetitive high schools.

Faced with those demographics, if not that prior history, there was every reason to believe that the outcome of the game in this instance would not be any different from those occurring in previous years between those two unequal football programs. And that is not even to consider that the "Little Lions" had an individual, playing at the quarterback position, who nearly every major college in the country was trying to recruit, including their nearby college namesake, the "Nittany Lions" of Penn State University, who, generally, played their football games in a much larger environment, called Beaver Stadium, on Saturday afternoons, as well.

Well, the "smaller lions," who played their games in a smaller stadium and on Friday evenings, too, seemed to have forgotten about the passing-skills of their very impressive quarterback, at least throughout the first half of that game, with only a few ineffectual exceptions in each of those two quarters, for rather short yardage gains, at most, in each instance. With a rather impressive line, at least in size, if not in numbers, they seemed to believe that they could simply "run all over," in football vernacular, their, seemingly, noncompetitive counterparts from Clinton County. In fact, with that in mind, one could safely say that they were rather one dimensional, offensively, that is, throughout that half, which may explain why they were not able to go anywhere, so to speak, not geographically, anyway, not in that half and not on that overly warm evening in early September in State College.

Actually, during the first "half of play," the "purple and white stalwarts," who were "manning" the line of scrimmage, were, realistically, if not uncharacteristically, immovable! Anchored by a gigantic "Moose," in the center of the line, and bordered on each side by the incomparable Bill Karch and Tom Toner, at left and right guard, respectively, it became like running into a stone wall, anywhere near that location, by several members of a disbelieving "lion-like-backfield." And when their more fleet footed colleagues tried to move slightly outside, nothing changed, not geographically, anyway, because they were confronted, at those wider points on the line of scrimmage, by a no less formidable duo of Dave Smith and Jack Roller, at left and right tackle, respectively. Finally, when they tried to "sweep the ends," as they often say in the game, more out of desperation than anything else, toward the end of the second quarter, waiting for them with "open arms," so to speak, was the indomitable Jan Bennett, playing at left end, and a no less formidable Wes Maggs, at the other end of that line!

Why "the smaller lions" became that one dimensional, by, essentially, trying to run through and, eventually, around, an immovable line, throughout an entire half, is, in retrospect, hard to explain, other than, possibly, by history. In that respect, "wearing down," as they like to say in the game, the other team's line, in a football game, especially where they happened to come from a smaller high school, with, correspondingly, limited backup players at each position, not unlike the one confronting them in that instance, seemed to work rather well in the past.

Nevertheless, it proved to be an historical practice that did not serve them very well in that half, and, believe it or not, they continued to rely on the same kind of practice in the second half, too, with only a few aerial interruptions, in each of those two quarters, having the same futile results, largely for the same immovable reasons on the line of scrimmage. In fact, that line was beginning to assume legendary proportions, at that point in the game, not unlike "The Seven Blocks of Granite," at Fordham University, immortalized, decades earlier, by the adroit pen of Timothy Cohane in 1936, according to a subsequent account by a local newspaper, known as, the *Lock Haven Express*.

Actually, with those unenviable results in mind, taking place over a four quarter period of time, one could safely say that a once proud group of "Little Lions" had become a football-playing group of "pussycats," which were unable to score on a "rock solid line," borrowing another football metaphor from Mr. Cohane, wearing, in this instance, however, "the purple and white uniform" of a "Bobcat!"

Meanwhile, Dave Johnson, playing at quarterback, John Englert, playing at fullback, and Bill Goodman and "Chub" Schiavo," playing at left and right halfback, respectively, were far more successful at "moving the ball," as they like to colloquially say in the game, than their "lion-like" counterparts.

Maybe not at first, however, because they, too, tried to run over and around an aroused "lion-of-a-line," clearly annoyed by all of that unpredictable difficulty occurring at the line of scrimmage and for nearly the entire first quarter, too. But the futility of continuing to do so, over the remainder of that quarter, proved to be lesson enough for Dave Johnson, still the quarterback of that rather ineffectual offense, at least up to that point, anyway. So with futility in mind, for nearly an entire quarter, that is, he decided to change his offensive strategy, by having John Englert throw a long pass to his left end, Jan Bennett, who, at that point in the game, was nearly thirty three yards down field, when he caught the ball, and on a dead run, too!

Interestingly enough, completing that pass to Jan Bennett, who was "well-covered," as they like to say in the game, by several players who were part of the opposing secondary, did not require a lot of difficulty, because he not over towered over both of them, but the rest of the players on that team as well.

Some of them, however, irrespective of their size, were nearly trampled to death, subsequently, by what appeared to be an enraged, "giraffe," on a partially obstructed way down the right sideline, all the way down to the opposing end zone, for a sixty seven yard score, on a completely surprised football team, which, at that point in the game, hardly looked like any "form of a lion."

Commencing their own series of downs, thereafter, following a nondescript kickoff return, the "smaller lions" were unable to even gain a first down, after three agonizing efforts to do so. Consequently, they kicked the ball on the fourth, to an unpredictable "purple and white phenomena," traveling all the way down to their twenty six yard line. But on the very first play thereafter, Kenny Miller, substituting at right halfback for a slightly injured "Chub" Schiavo, succeeded in "turning the corner," as it has been often said in games like that, around the right side of an opposing line. And, thereafter, he ran right past several members of a, seemingly, stunned secondary, which looked, at that point in the game, like a group of "stationary lions," if not totally surprised ones, for a seventy four yard touchdown dash, to, essentially, end the first half, minutes later. And with two successful extra points, kicked by none other than John Edward Englert, the score, by the end of that half, the first half of that football game, was, surprisingly, "fourteen to nothing," in favor of the smaller high school from the smaller town in the far more rural and economically challenged, neighboring, Clinton County.

Likely disheartened, if not disoriented, by the score at halftime, a distinctly "wounded lion" was not the same kind of a "jungle cat," in the third quarter, not even remotely the same. That probably explains why, "The Boys From Across The River," were able to march down the field, nearly the entire field, right after the opening kickoff, virtually unimpeded, or ineffectively so, until they were able to reach the seven yard line of a, seemingly, crippled adversary. At that critical point, a smaller version of the "king of the jungle," stiffened, at least for two downs, allowing no more than a few yards on each try. Whereupon, Bill Goodman, still playing at left halfback, executed a "coup de grace," on the third, by running right through a gaping hole in the defensive line of those "miniature lions," compliments of a gigantic "Moose." And by doing so, he sealed the "purple and white effort," to accomplish an historic change in the outcome of football games between those two dissimilar high schools, not to mention their surrounding towns and counties.

The remainder of that quarter, which, of course, was the third quarter of that football game, as well as the one that followed, really became somewhat inconsequential, at least with respect to the final score. Nevertheless, for your possible interest, the entire fourth quarter was played "between the stripes," in the ancient language of the game, demarcating the twenty one and forty eight yard line of a rapidly deteriorating football team, which was anything but "lion-like," not at that point in the game, anyway. And lest we forget, the final score of "twenty points," by an astounding team from a smaller high school in a smaller town, located in a neighboring county, rural and poor in comparison, included two extra points, kicked in the "first half of play," as they characteristically say in the game, by what would eventually become the continually versatile and prolific John Edward Englert. Unfortunately, however, Dave Johnson missed an extra point kick following the touchdown in the second half, which, apparently, explains why he was never used in that capacity again, not in the following games that season. Notwithstanding that extra point failure, the score at the end of the game remained "twenty," for the unpredictably impressive "Bobcats," to "nothing," for the overly confident and, eventually, embarrassed "Little Lions."

In the end, the lack of any points scored by a normally impressive football team from a distinctly larger high school, located in an urban borough, in a far more affluent county, was historically, sociologically and demographically inexplicable, at least seemingly so at the time, but not for all time, however, certainly not by the end of that season. No, by the end of that season, the reasons had become legendary, as the indescribable line-play, among a number of other notable things, or factors, over that period of time, by a Karch, a Houser, a Toner, a Maggs, a Roller, a Smith and a Bennett, who, journalistically, became known as "The Seven Blocks of Granite," in the words borrowed, once again, from the earlier, useful, language of Timothy Cohane.

But I hasten to point out that, "The Seven Blocks of Granite" were forged, in this instance, across the West Branch of the Susquehanna River, in and among the Appalachian Mountains, from whence they came, the legend-makers, I mean. And that legend, when it eventually became one, had its origins in the inexplicable drubbing of an overly confident group of "Little Lions," who could not even score, not once, not during the entire four quarters of that surprising football game!

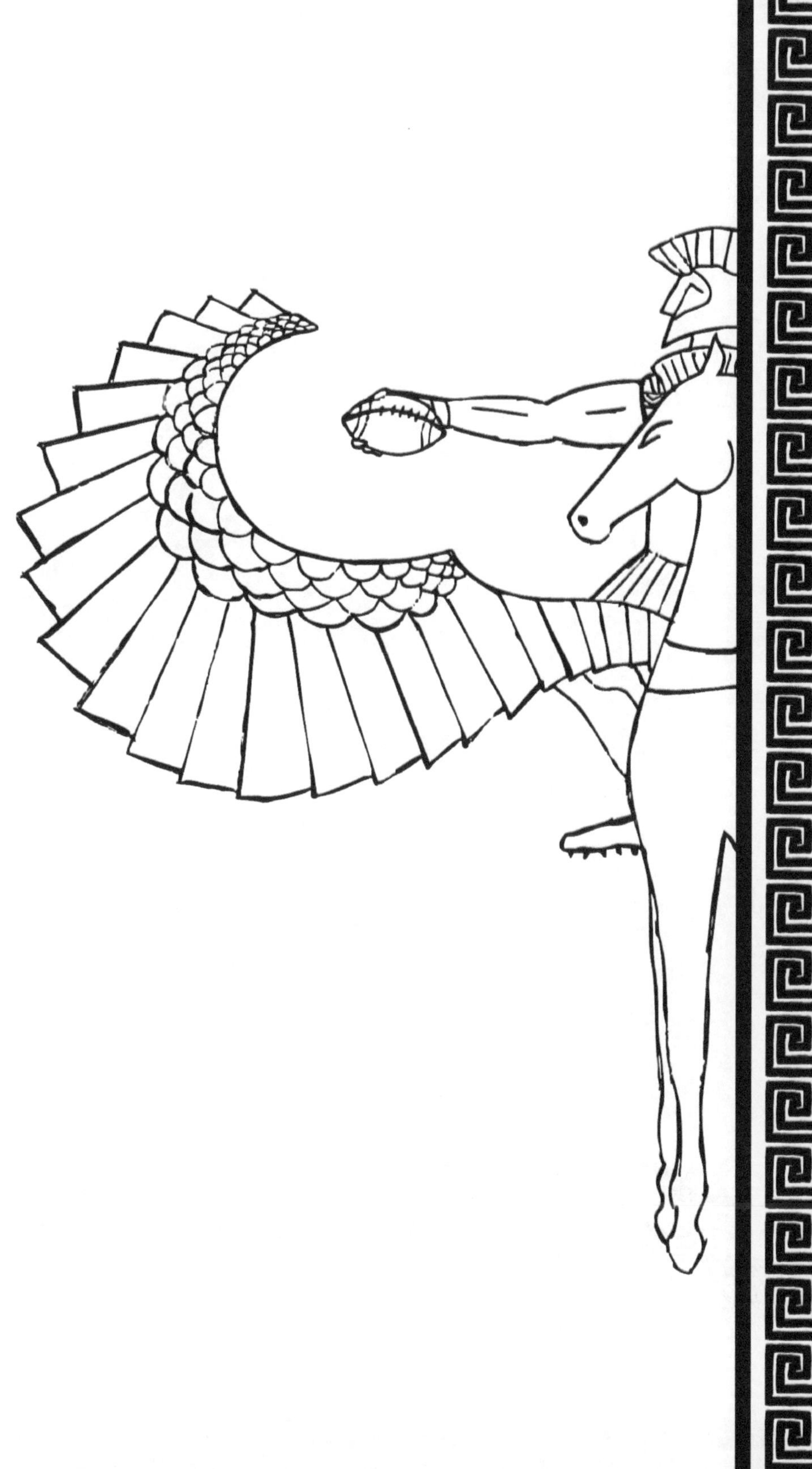

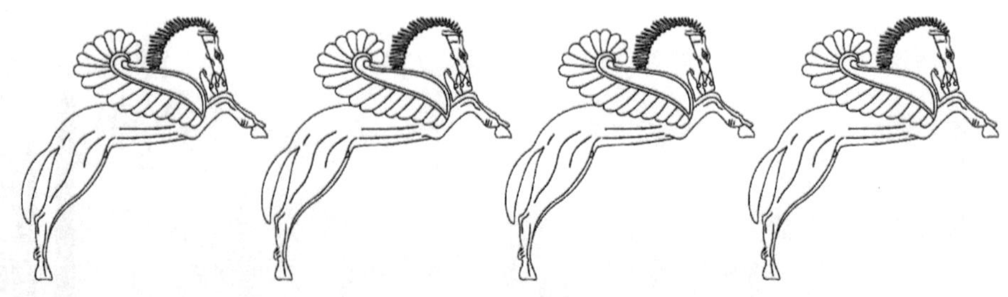

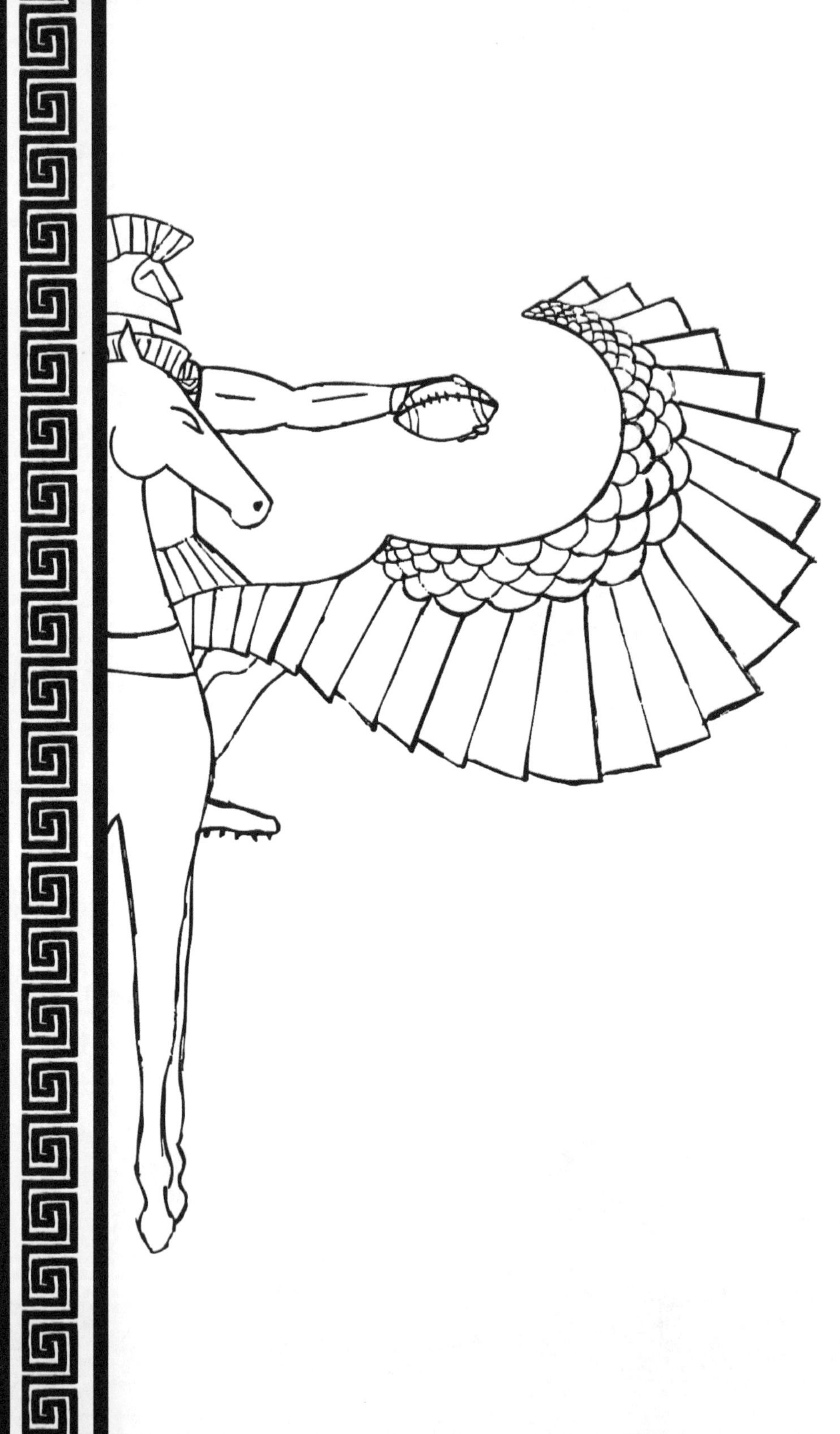

THE SECOND GAME

CONFRONTING MORE THAN THE "ORANGE AND BLACK" OF THE JERSEY SHORE HIGH SCHOOL "BULLDOGS," FOR ECONOMIC, SOCIOLOGIC AND GEOGRAPHIC REASONS, IF NOT FOR OTHER SEEMING SIMILARITIES, IN THE SECOND GAME OF THE SEASON, "THE BOYS FROM ACROSS THE RIVER," AS THEY HAD BECOME KNOWN BY THAT TIME, NARROWLY PREVAILED IN AN UNCOMFORTABLE VICTORY, FOR ALL OF THE FOREGONE REASONS, BY THE UNSEEMLY SCORE OF "FOURTEEN TO NOTHING," LARGELY AS A RESULT OF THE LEGENDARY PLAY OF "THE SEVEN BLOCKS OF GRANITE."

HAVING BEEN victorious over the fabled, "Little Lions," a week ago, "The Boys From Across The River," as they had become known by that time, traveled, northeastwardly, down Route 220, in a dilapidated, yellow school bus, once again, to confront more than the "Orange and Black" of the Jersey Shore High School "Bulldogs."

That qualified confrontational conclusion was predicated upon the fact that those "doggish-players" were really not unlike "The Boys From Across The River; and, moreover, their respective student bodies were not at all dissimilar, either. That was likely because of the geographical proximity of their respective schools, not to mention the residences of their respective student bodies, and the sociological consequences arising therefrom.

In fact, some of the students in each school may have been distantly related to some of those in the other school; or, at least, they may have been friends, or, possibly, friends of friends. And they may have even been patients of the same dentists or doctors in the area; or they may have been associated with each other in other respects, such as membership in the same church, largely because of their geographical proximity and their similar sociological circumstances, as a result thereof, if you do not mind those repetitive facts.

For all of those sociological and geographical reasons, if not the familial ones, too, it is not at all difficult to conclude that, at the very least, many of the respective students in each one of those two high schools likely knew some of those who were attending the other high school, too. And not inconsistent therewith, it is just as likely that, at the very least, many of the respective football players on each one of those two teams likely knew some of those who were playing on the other team, too, which, not surprisingly, made the athletic contest somewhat complicated . . . to them and to their respective student bodies, too!

That season did not prove to be an exception, either, not to any one of those complicating circumstances, not for all of those geographical and sociological reasons. And if they were not complicating enough, in and of themselves, the Jersey Shore High School "Bulldogs" also had quarterback from "across the river," too, who decided to become a, "Bulldog," instead of a "Bobcat." And because of their shared geographic origins, if nothing else, he and Dave Johnson, the quarterback for the "Bobcats," had become rather good friends during their formative years, but not, necessarily, on that complicated Friday evening!

No, on that complicated evening, "The Seven Blocks of Granite" were far more immobile on defense than their "canine counterparts" on the line of scrimmage. Likely for those "immobile" reasons, the "canine quarterback" said, following the game, that the opposing left guard, Bill Karch, was in his backfield, "chasing him around back there," for most of the game. Maybe that was a partial explanation for his team's inability to cross their own forty nine yard line, except on one occasion, over the entire four quarters of that football game. And that occasion occurred because one of them, who even looked like a "bulldog," except that he was outfitted in a "black and orange uniform," serendipitously recovered a fumble on the "purple and white" thirty two yard line.

It became the only glimmer of hope on an otherwise depressing evening for the hometown crowd, wearing, of course, their "orange and black sweatshirts," and a visible frown upon their expectant faces, as well, over the entire game. Unfortunately, however, hope was about the only thing that sprang from that fumble recovery, because, notwithstanding a "dogged-effort," over all four downs, no less, not much changed, not geographically, anyway, because those "orange and black bulldogs" were unable to go anywhere, not thereafter, not of any consequence, anyway!

It became, in that respect, a frustrating evening for those poor "Bulldogs," not only because of a "cat-like defense," anchored by a rapidly developing "granite-like legend;" but, also, and just as importantly, because of an unstoppable offense, courtesy of a Johnson, an Englert, a Schiavo and a Goodman, who were, in the opinion of a local journalist, not unlike the fearsome-foursome, playing, years ago, at Notre Dame, and eulogized, at the time, as "The Four Horsemen," by the continuously adroit pen of Grantland Rice.

Adopting that metaphor, with, admittedly, less than an adroit pen, "The Four Horsemen," in this instance, initiated their offense with a, surprising, seventeen yard pass by Dave Johnson, in the first quarter, to a gigantic "giraffe," misnamed "Bennett," at least off the football field, measuring more in feet than in pounds, who, literally, towered over his immediate environment, which, in that instance, happened to be several members of a, hapless, "canine secondary."

Catching the ball with relative ease, all six feet seven inches of that "giraffe" immediately began lumbering down the field, as those kinds of creatures are inclined to do, with his newly acquired possession tucked firmly under one arm. And, eventually, finding himself without enemies, or even friends, at a crucial point on the field, that long-legged, "left end," if you prefer the more traditional football terminology, simply continued the rest of the way down the field, without too much trouble, or even causing the same. That is, if, by chance, you are inclined to overlook the chorus of boisterous laughter by his hysterical teammates at the unfamiliar sight of that, strangely, moving figure, "playing out," as they say, on that semi-empty part of the football field.

Not much else transpired over the rest of that half, not by way of scoring or scampering, because "The Four Horsemen" . . . so named, as you may recall, because of a seeming similarity to their earlier, collegiate, counterparts at Notre Dame . . . could not, successfully, mount much of a running game, not thereafter, not against a slightly unnerved, but, still, quite proud group of neighboring "Bull Dogs." And, now, continually aware of the whereabouts of the "giraffe," because of both his height and history, at least at that point in the game, the "canine critters," residing in the secondary of that opposing team, refused to let him out of their sight, which, given his height, was not at all a tall order. So somewhat stymied for the remainder of that half, to the relief of the hometown crowd, the visiting "feline relatives," or, at least, "cat-like friends," not to mention their "doggish-hosts," trotted off the field, at the conclusion thereof, with only one score, by a pass to a certifiable giant. And, consequently, a lead of seven uncomfortable points, at that point in the game, scored by, at the very least, their former friends, from down the road, one of which being the contribution of an almost mechanical, extra point kick, by none other than the very capable Mr. Englert!

Interestingly, not much changed in the third quarter, either, not for either one of those two frustrated teams, likely for the same defensive, if not interrelated, reasons. And it began to look like a surprising aerial score was going to be the only difference between those two teams, or those two neighbors, or those two former friends, who were so associated, demographically and geographically, that it was almost a sociological impossibility to engage in the confrontation in the first place, let alone to add to the discomfort of one of them by that score!

Notwithstanding that discomforting potential, if not that perennial, sociological problem, shortly before the fourth quarter ended, with the end of the game nearly in sight, Bill Goodman, playing at left halfback for the, maddening, "Bobcats," at least at that point in the game, added to the frustrating score, and to everyone's discomfort, for, obviously, differing reasons, by disappearing into the line of scrimmage, in what appeared to only be a short yardage effort. But all of a sudden, he emerged on the other side, "the canine side," for no apparent reason, and, thereafter, managing to avoid every one of those "dog-like linebackers," one after the other, while outrunning their two safeties, at nearly the same time, he, eventually, ended the scoring by either team, with the possible exception of an extra point, added, once again, by the ever-reliable, kicking foot of John Edward Englert.

Following that disconcerting conclusion to a, distinctly, local confrontation, if not a neighborly one, "The Boys From Across The River" left that familiar stadium with an uncomfortable victory, because, in the long run, it may have resulted in the loss of some friends, if not some distant relatives, and, possibly, the affection of a number of their neighbors in, nearby, Lycoming County. Nevertheless, they managed to quickly board a dilapidated, yellow school bus, once again, even though it was for a rather uncomfortable trip back home, not because of the bus ride, or the trip, itself, which was nothing more than a fifteen mile "trek," back down Route 220, but because of a disquieting football victory over the "Black and Orange" of the Jersey Shore High School "Bulldogs, by an, unseemly, score of "fourteen to nothing."

I wonder, as I conclude the description of that game, whether "The Boys From Across The River" had any idea about what had just happened, apart from the score and the disquieting consequences, that is. And, moreover, that it would happen again and again, in the weeks that follow, sometimes in far more challenging circumstances, largely due to the size of the opposing high school and, largely, for the same explicable, if not inexplicable, reasons. And, significantly, both of those kind of reasons had already begun to reach beyond the parameters of that game, or, rather, those two games, and, thereby, assume proportions that were becoming legendary in the folklore that was beginning to arise in those mountainous regions.

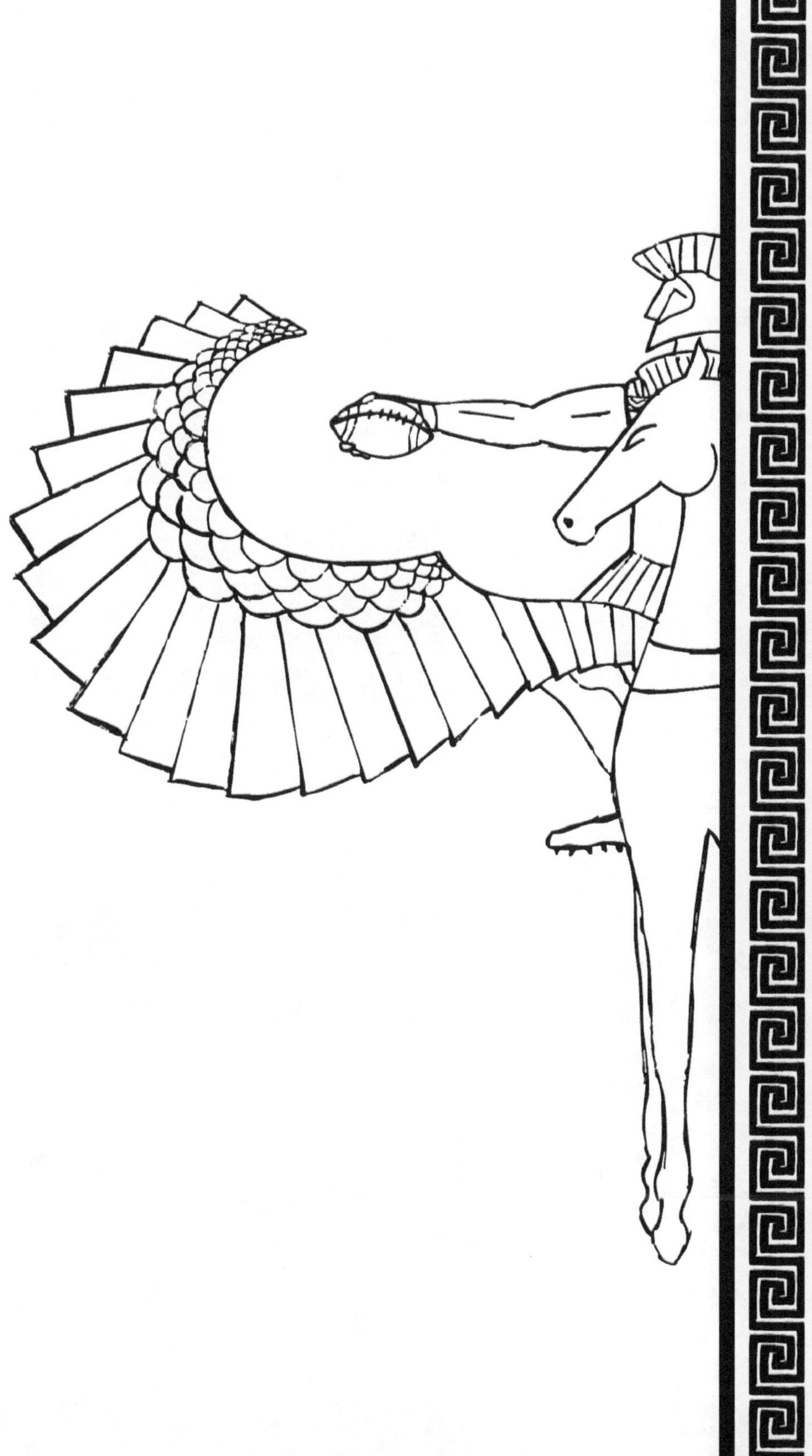

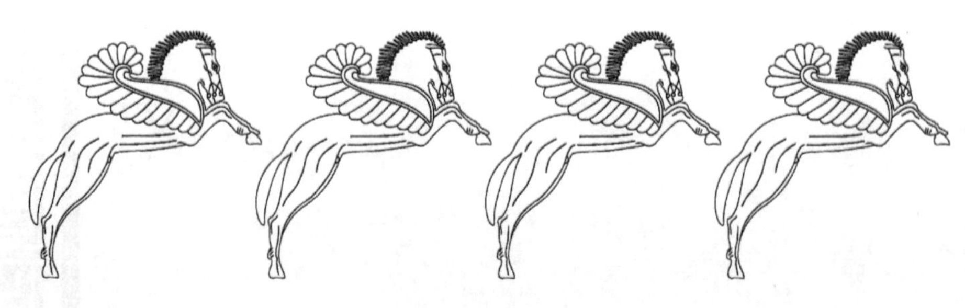

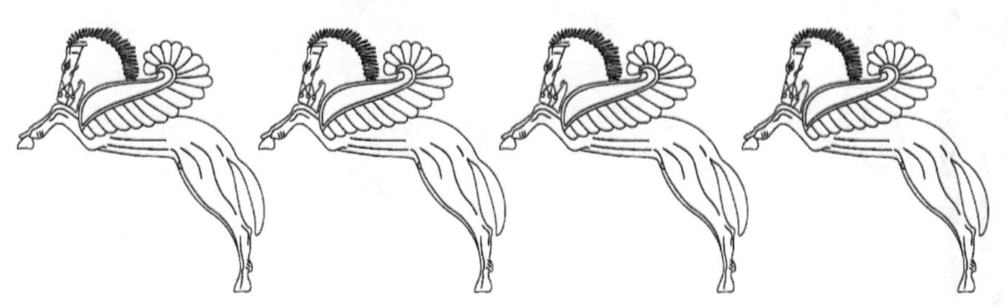

THE THIRD GAME

THE LEGENDARY PLAY OF "THE BOYS FROM ACROSS THE RIVER" IN THE GAME BETWEEN THE LOCK HAVEN HIGH SCHOOL "BOBCATS" AND THE "RED RAIDERS" OF BELLEFONTE HIGH SCHOOL, WHICH WAS THE THIRD GAME OF THE SEASON, HAD THE DEMORALIZING IMPACT OF AN APOCALYPSE DESCENDING UPON THE POOR "RED RAIDERS," OVER ALL FOUR QUARTERS OF THAT GAME, WHICH, BY THE WAY, ENDED BY THE, OTHERWORLDLY, SCORE OF "THIRTY-THREE" FOR THE "DEMONIC DUDES" FROM LOCK HAVEN HIGH SCHOOL AND ONLY "THIRTEEN" FOR THE "BEWITCHED BOYS" FROM BELLEFONT HIGH SCHOOL.

On the following Friday evening, the undefeated "Red Raiders" from Bellefonte High School came to town, in order to confront a growing legend about the incredible play of an undefeated and untied football team, at least at that point in the season, on its home-turf at the J. Arlington Painter Stadium. And, moreover, the "Red

Raiders" refused to be intimidated by the untied and undefeated season, or the rapidly developing legend with respect thereto, or even the reasons therefor, not initially, anyway, not on that evening and not on that field, even though it was on the field of those who had earned them all.

In fact, the "raiding party in red" managed to "drive down the field," as they say in the game, with only a modicum of difficulty, upon receiving the opening kickoff to commence the first quarter. And they, eventually, managed to score on a, formerly, unyielding, but, now, slightly discombobulated, "wall of granite," at least at that overly confident point in the season, on their way to putting an end to growing legends, as well as undefeated and untied seasons, if not the reasons therefor. Moreover, near the end of the fourth quarter and the end of the game, the "raiding-party" did it again, by "marching right down the field," as they still say in the game, for a, virtually, unobstructed score. Unlike the earlier one, however, occurring, as you may recall, in the first quarter of the game, this one occurred against a junior varsity eleven, which had entered the game, long after it had been "put out of reach," as they still say in the game, by the scoring proficiency, over all four quarters, of a Schiavo, an Englert, a Goodman and a Johnson, or, if you will, "The Four Horsemen," in the currently applicable words of Grantland Rice.

It all began . . . their scoring, I mean . . . right after that surprising touchdown by the "Red Raiders," to commence the first quarter of the game. Thereafter, following an unimpressive return of a kickoff, "The Four Horsemen" went to work, so to speak, by, methodically, "moving the ball," in the colloquial language of the game, in running play after running play, inside and outside of a stunned defensive line, right down to their eighteen yard line, with very little trouble at all. At that pivotal point, Bill Goodman, still playing at left halfback and known, at the time, as "Mr. Inside," largely in the hometown newspaper, maneuvered his way through the interior of the "raider line," quite successfully, I might add. And before anyone in a "reddish uniform" had any conceivable way of stopping him, he was scampering down one of the sidelines, on his way to, what would eventually become, a distinctly "one sided affair," in the common place language of most journalists. Interestingly enough, John Englert capped off that "march," not to mention that "remarkable run," in his own inimical way, by, automatically, kicking an extra point thereafter. And with that, "The Boys From Across The River" had succeeded in tying the score, at "seven to seven," midway through the first quarter.

Although both teams made a serious effort to change that score throughout the remainder of that quarter, the first quarter of that football game, neither one had any success in doing so. Near the end of the quarter, however, the "Purple and White" appeared to have scored again, on a very long pass by Englert to Bennett, who towered over everything on that field, born of man and woman, irrespective of the nature of their uniforms, or even the color thereof; unfortunately, however, that touchdown was "called back," as they say in the language of the game, because of an offside penalty by an overzealous "Moose."

Shortly after the second quarter began, however, "The Four Horsemen" began to "ride again," borrowing another applicable metaphor from Grantland Rice, on another one of their unstoppable "marches down the field," as has been said so often in the game. And it did not end, by the way, until Bill Goodman, still playing at left halfback, stumbled into the end zone, on an "off-tackle play," as they descriptively say in the game. Thereby, completing the aspirations, on that drive, of the highly performing "Purple and White," at the expense of the under performing "Red and White," at least at that point in the contest.

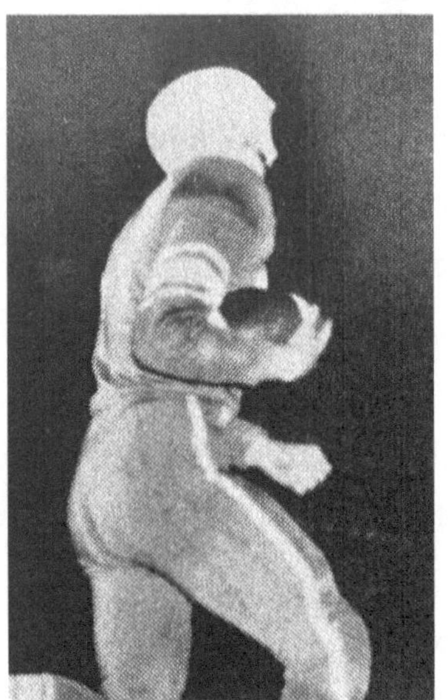

Following that inartful score, nothing over the remainder of that second quarter seemed to be working out for "the boys" from "the beautiful fountain," which, by the way, was a descriptive phrase employed by its, supposed, French Founder, Talleyrand, in describing a town otherwise known, in far more contemporary circumstances, as "Bellefonte." As a result, "The Boys From Across The River" "left the field," as they say, at the conclusion of the first half, slightly ahead of the "Red Raiders," by a "thirteen to seven" score. And that was notwithstanding an aberrational failure on the part of the normally reliable Mr. Englert to secure an extra point, following that last touchdown.

In the second half, however, there did not seem to be anything on that field, "outfitted in a red and white uniform," which was capable of stopping that offense, maybe not anything in the Conference, maybe not anything in the State, maybe not anything in the Nation, maybe not even anything on the "Earth," not at the time, anyway. And for the first time, over the course of that challenging season, it began to appear that the legendary nature of that highly unusual football team did not stop, as previously supposed, at the line of scrimmage. And with that, the names of Schiavo, Goodman, Englert and Johnson began to become part of the narrative, too, as, subsequently, identifiable as the names of "The Seven Blocks of Granite," in the folklore that was beginning to arise, off the field, in those mountainous areas.

Indeed, following the opening kickoff to the "red men," to commence the second half, their quarterback, on the second play from the line of scrimmage, lofted an errant throw, landing, mistakenly and injudiciously, into the overly broad arms of a John Edward Englert. And he, immediately, took advantage of the surprising situation, by returning that interception nearly fifty seven yards, for yet another score, seemingly before anyone on either team could fully comprehend what had just happened! The whole serendipitous thing must have had a disquieting effect on his, normally, laid-back demeanor, however, because he, subsequently, missed the extra point kick, going wide of the upright, likely for just that reason, according to an editorial comment, on the following day, in the

hometown newspaper. Even in that absence, however, the score at that point in the contest, which was early in the second half, became "nineteen," for the astounding "Purple and White," and just "six," for the less than impressive "Red and White!"

Following the inability of the "Red Raiders" to, essentially, "move the ball," thereafter, in the lexicon of the game, the "purple and white juggernaut," not at all hyperbole at that point in the second half, began their next offensive series on their own forty eight yard line. That excellent field position, or their good fortune, if you want to think about it in that manner, was the result of a "bungled punt," in a less widely use of the lexicon, by a subsequently embarrassed kicker in "red and white," not excluding his uncomfortable visage. On the other hand, "The Four Horsemen" began to seem, at that point on the field, if not at that point in the game, to have, effectively, descended from the cataclysmic promises of the Biblical "Apocalypse!"

Confirming that hellish suspicion, from an advantageous point on the field now, they resumed their methodical, if not maniacal, "march down the field," if you do not mind an overly used phrase in the game, all over again and without too much trouble. Finally, at the eight yard line, belonging to a visibly disturbed group of "red and white football players," the "devil's henchman," himself, in the football form of "Chub" Schiavo, still playing at right halfback in that diabolical game, took a direct snap from an "inhuman center," at least virtually, given those gigantic proportions, especially for high school athlete. And with two "pulling-demons" in front of him, otherwise known as "guards," in the more traditional football parlance, he immediately avoided two or three linemen and, subsequently, several linebackers, too, all of whom were "outfitted in red and white," while making a, virtually, "clean sweep," in the same kind of parlance, around the left side of that visually disturbed line, which, as a result thereof, had become somewhat ineffectual at that point in the second half of the game.

Following that clever, if not outlandish, maneuver, he finished a demonically driven run, or so it seemed, right through an astonished secondary, whose, questionably, hesitant response seemed to indicate that they had just seen a "ghost." And, finally, he ended that, seemingly, otherworld spectacle, or incredible run, depending upon your imagination, by, jauntily, entering a "red and white end zone," literally untouched by human hands, but not, necessarily, by other kinds, in the astonished opinion of a journalist in the hometown newspaper on the following day.

The unimaginable result, of course, was yet another score by an undefeated and untied football team, or something like it, according to the same journalist, which seemed, at least to him, to have become "unstoppable," at that point in the game, if not at that point in the season, at least by "human hands," on that frightful Friday evening in October. Oh, yes, lest we forget, the score, which, by now, was becoming outlandish, was followed by an extra point kick by the, seemingly, unnatural toe of John Edward Englert, in the opinion of the same journalist at that point in the game, if not at that point in the season. Forgetting about an, earlier, aberration in that respect, the score had now become, at the end of the third quarter, an unreachable, "twenty six," as the result of the unearthly behavior of "The Four Horsemen," to a paltry "seven," in the absence thereof, by the other, more humanly flawed, football team, outfitted, of course, in a, now, somewhat paler, if not shaky, "red and white."

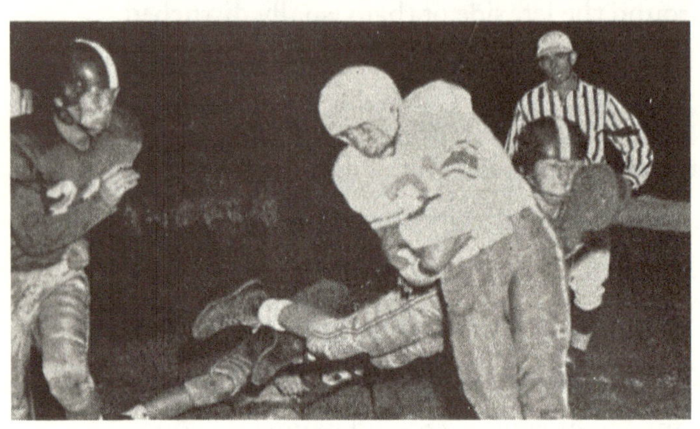

If you are still wondering, however, that was not the end of the "Apocalypse," metaphorically, if not Biblically, descending upon those poor fellows from the historic city to the southwest, named by a wayward Frenchman, "la belle fonte," or "Bellefonte," in the pervading English translation. In that respect, "The Four Horsemen," or, at least, one of them, still playing at left halfback, broke through a, thoroughly, "demoralized line" . . . the adjective of which happens to be an etymological concept, so I am informed, derived from the horrors of the French Revolution . . . trampled several members of a "red and white secondary," thereafter, who, being visibly shaken, were likely aware of that terrifying etymology. And in a fiendish fashion, or so I am told, he literally outran nearly everything else on the field that hailed from there, or as one journalist subsequently suggested, maybe even from hell!

Although the score at that point was beginning to become an embarrassment . . . not just to the Frenchman, "Talleyrand," but, likely, to all seven of the former governors, who had, once, resided in that historic city . . . the Coach, nevertheless, decided to send another "demon" onto the field, in the football form of John Edward Englert, to kick an extra point, which he did; or as the same journalist subsequently suggested, in the hometown newspaper, something did! As a result, the score, at the end of that one-sided affair, had become a miraculous, "thirty three," for the "demonic dudes" from Lock Haven High School, and a paltry "seven" for the "bewitched boys" from Bellefonte High School!

It would become the last score by a, seemingly, surreal backfield, whose unearthly membership was the subject of an editorial discussion, on the very next day, by nearly every sports editor in the area. Some of whom concluded that all four of them were actually "unreal," if not "hellishly so," and not just in their "indescribable play," either. Included in that "over the top" assessment, which, journalistically, continued, in one form or another, throughout that disbelieving season, was the fact that, in the editors subsequent notations, Bellefonte would not lose another game that season, and "certainly not by a score like that!" Indeed, as it was subsequently noted, in that respect, the "Red Raiders" had never "been beaten that badly in a football game," not that anyone of them could actually remember, anyway, "not for years," they conjectured!

With all of that in mind, as well as the eerie similarity to their "play" in all of their previous games, not to mention the unpredictable outcome in one of them, given the formidable nature of that opposing team, there was something "outlandish," in the minds of many of those editors, about a football team that had become known, "far-and-wide," as "The Boys From Across The River," which was hard to explain, other than by "otherworldly terms."

Well, returning to more worldly considerations, in that disbelieving football game, occurring over the last quarter of that one-sided game, it had become "so far out of reach," as they say, by the

"Red Raiders," as a result of the, seemingly, "Mephistophelian" play of "The Boys From Across The River," that their Coach decided to retire that terrifying varsity, darkly so, for the remainder of that unreal game. I am speaking here of "The Four Horsemen," possibly descended from the "Apocalypse," according to some of those newspaper accounts, and their demonically driven brothers on that stout-hearted line, journalistically known as "The Seven Blocks of Granite," in the current use of another football metaphor, coined, as you already know by now, by none other than Grantland Rice. Thereafter, both of those groups of fearsome football players, linemen as well as backfield, became "unnatural spectators," in the minds of many of those journalists, in their heavily worn, if not severely blemished, "purple and white uniforms," for the remainder of the fourth quarter!

Accordingly, the rest of the game, as I have previously reported, but in a different context, was actually played between an excited junior varsity, largely because they were able to get into the game, at least at that point, especially in their crispy-clean, "purple and white uniforms," and a dispirited varsity, largely because they were not able to get out of the game, and, even worse, their former, "roguish red uniforms" were now more "grassy green" than "raider red." And notwithstanding those distinctions, or, possibly, because of them, the rest of the game, taking place over the remainder of that fourth quarter, was not much to talk about, other than in colors or the lack thereof, so I won't, not at this point, anyway. Instead, I will simply note that, by the time that quarter had ended, which, of course, was the last quarter of the game, the rather blemished colors of the varsity were able to score on the unblemished colors of the junior varsity, which was not at all surprising, given the nature of those two units, giving the "bewitched boys" from Bellefonte, that historic town in Centre County, another "six points."

Nevertheless, by the end of that hair-raising affair, "The Boys From Across The River" were victorious once again; this time by the ungodly score of "thirty three," for those who had, seemingly, appeared out of the enigmatic aspects of the Appalachian Mountains, in order to cross the West Branch of the Susquehanna River, so that they could enlist in the "devil's play," on a scholastic gridiron on a Friday evening in central Pennsylvania, according to the some of the more hyperbolic editors; and, of course, only "thirteen," for those who had not!

But in reality, if not in all honesty, something else seemed to have happened in that game, which was inexplicable and which may have transcended that lopsided score, if not the game itself. And it may have transcended time and games and Friday evenings, too, even though it had become legendarily apparent in those games and on those Friday evenings. And that legendary aspect would eventually become folklore, long before "timelessness" would ever become part of the athletic equation, and mythical, when it subsequently did, years later.

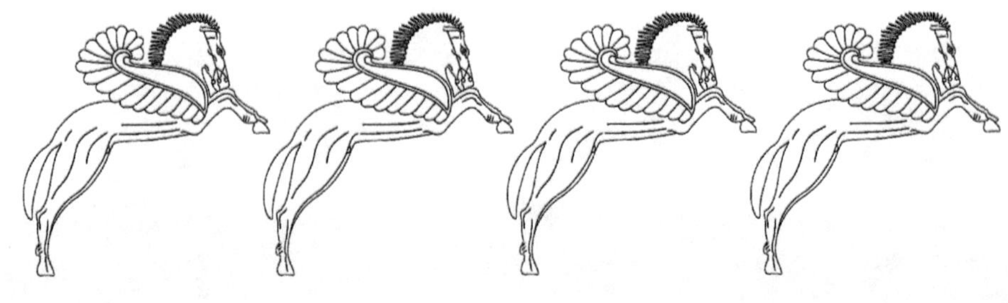

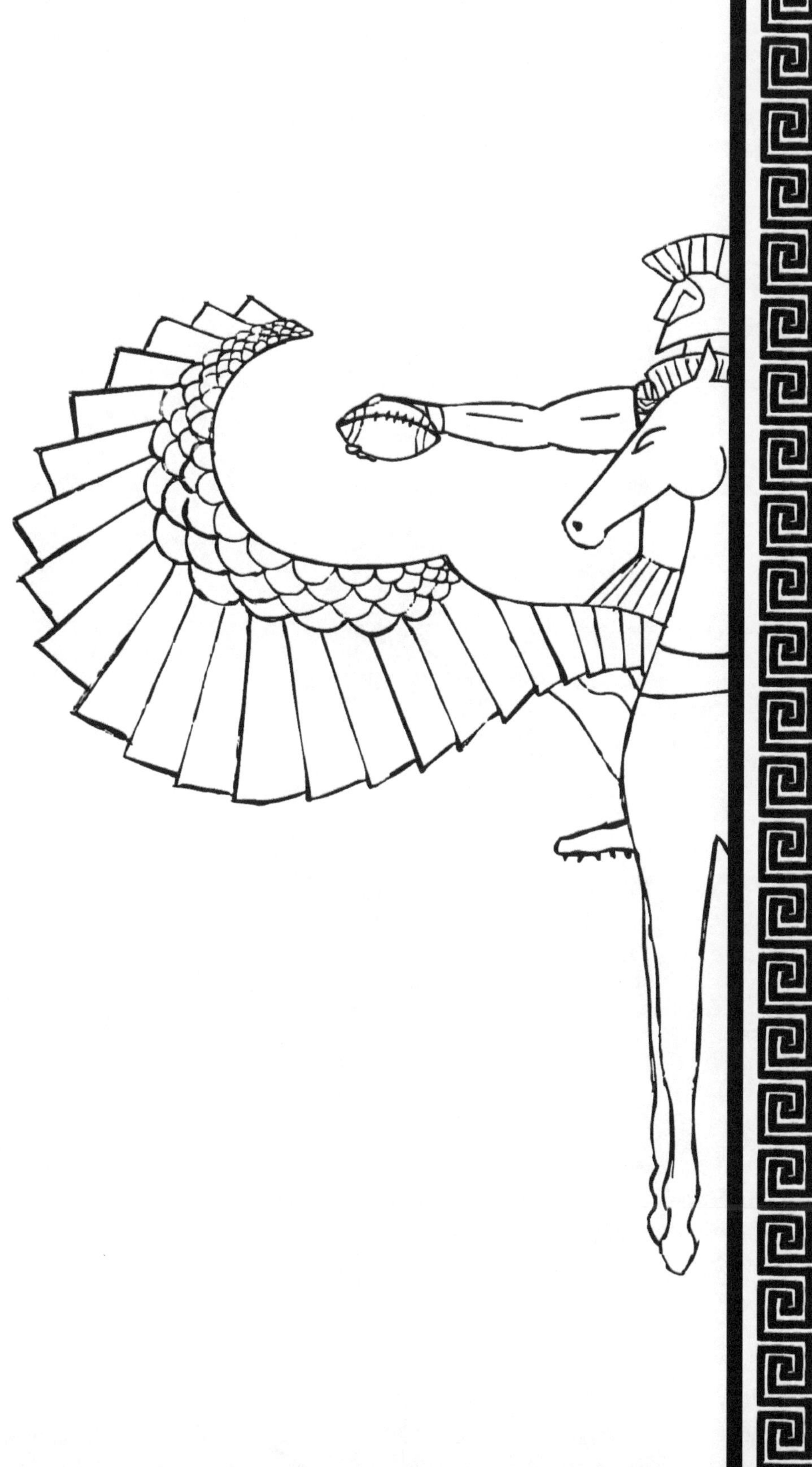

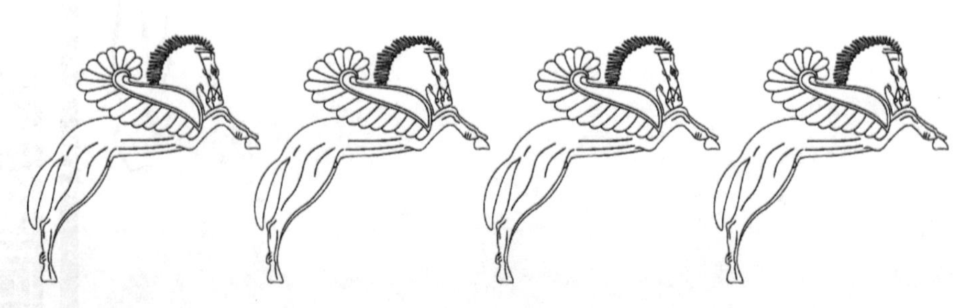

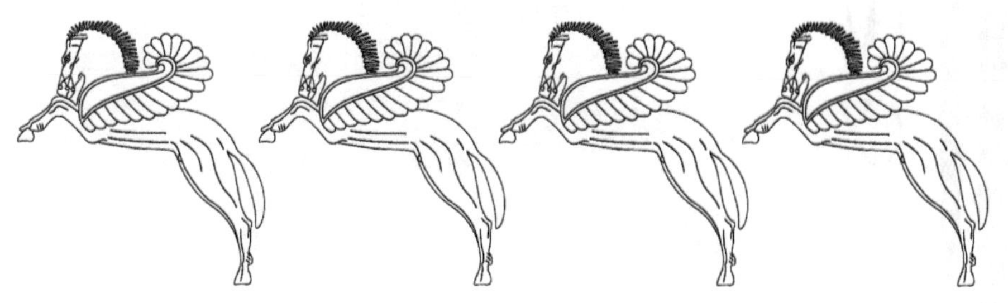

THE FOURTH GAME

THE VICTORY OF THE LOCK HAVEN HIGH SCHOOL OVER THE LARGER HUNTINGTON HIGH SCHOOL, IN THE FOURTH FOOTBALL GAME OF THE SEASON, BECAME LEGENDARY AT THE TIME AND FOLKLORE SUBSEQUENT THERETO, BECAUSE OF THE DISSIMILARITIES BETWEEN THOSE TWO HIGH SCHOOLS, WHICH, SEEMINGLY, FAVORED THE HUNTINGTON HIGH SCHOOL "BEARCATS."

On the following Friday evening, "The Boys From Across The River" traveled, southwestwardly, all the way over the Allegheny Mountains, in their dilapidated, yellow school bus, once again, to face a far more formidable foe, the "Red and Dark Blue" of the Huntington High School "Bearcats," in the fourth game of that season, who were part of a conference of much larger high schools in the western part of the State, known as the mighty Western Conference. In fact, the only high school in that Conference that even approached the size of their own, smaller, high school was the Huntington High School. And even that westerly school was substantially larger, which probable explains why the games were annually played in that stadium, rather than in their own, with a perennial score, thereafter, which was just as unfavorable to the "Bobcats." Because of that perennial loss, not to mention the laborious trip in just getting there, the hometown newspaper editorially questioned the judgment displayed by the local high school officials, every year, in even scheduling a larger high school like that from a powerful conference like that and in their very own stadium, too.

Those editorial concerns were unnecessary on this southwesterly trip, however, because that dilapidated, yellow school bus made the trip with "The Seven Blocks of Granite." And for four frustrating quarters, the vaunted, "red and dark blue machine," found those "granite-like structures," shoring up a, comparatively, undersized-line, to be absolutely immovable! Indeed, the "bear like cats," for want of a better name, could not even find their way across the "purple and white" forty four yard line, with two inconsequential exceptions, resulting from an intercepted pass, in one instance, and a fumble recovery in the other. Both of which proved to be relatively immaterial, however, because the "red and dark blue offense" found it to be no more hospitable on that, unfamiliar, side of the football field!

Meanwhile, being a bit more hospitable, but not much more, the defensive line of those "bearish cats" gave ground, although reluctantly so, in a "methodical drive," as they like to say in the game, over a series-of-downs, by "The Four Horsemen," near the end of the first half. And although they became mired down at the two yard line of the "red and dark blue," following two unsuccessful passing efforts, they were finally able to score by "handing the ball off," as they like to say in the game, to a "diving dervish," otherwise known in more polite circles, generally found off of the football field, as Bill Goodman, still playing at the left halfback position at the time.

Following that "hard won success," as they like to say in the game, John Englert, amazingly, missed the extra point try, by a kick meandering wide of the goal posts, which, in itself, may have been more noteworthy at that point in the game, if not at that point in the season, than the score, itself. Nevertheless, noteworthy or not, "The Boys From Across The River" were now ahead of the Hunting High School "Bearcats," by a more than surprising score of "six to nothing," by the end of the first half!

Moreover, not much changed in the second half, neither on the field nor on the scoreboard, for that strangely-named football team, called the "Bearcats." They continued to be frustrated, geographically and arithmetically, by the unyielding play on the line of scrimmage of the "Seven Blocks of Granite, over both of those two final quarters. For that frustrating reason, they simply could not muster much of an offense, not at any point during those two quarters, not over the entire second half. But I can't say the same thing about the team from a smaller high school, which had already scored in the first half, called the "Bobcats!"

In fact, the second half actually began with Bob Crissman . . . substituting, briefly, for a slightly injured Bill Goodman, at left halfback . . . returning the ensuing kickoff nearly eighty four yards, by bobbing and weaving his way up the left side line, all the way up to midfield, with a lot of missed tackles in between. With the goal line now clearly in sight, about forty-six yards away, he decided to change direction, ever so slightly, at that point on the field, in order to confuse those who were still pursuing him. And, finally, with a relatively clear path in front of him, having left most of those "bear like cats" behind, he decided to head straight down the remainder of the field toward the goal line.

Subsequently crossing it, relatively unscathed and, seemingly, "no worse for the wear," as they often say at that point in the game, not on his "purple and white jersey," anyway, he ambled, slowly and confidently, over to his team's partially empty "bench," not even "winded," as they are also prone to say in such, obviously, trying circumstances. Joined now by the rest of his teammates for a welcome respite, while the game "officials were having some kind of a discussion, he was clearly overwhelmed by their hearty congratulations!

At the conclusion thereof, John Englert arose from the "bench," and he slowly walked out onto the field, as was his custom, in order to successfully kick an extra point, which was also his custom!

The rest of that quarter, and most of the fourth, were, essentially, reduced to a, so-called, "cat and mouse game," as they say in almost in context, between the "boys in red and dark blue" and the "boys in purple and white." Because neither one of those two multicolored outfits seemed to be able to do much better, arithmetically or, even, geographically, during that challengingly period of time, no matter what they tried, not until the fourth quarter and the game had nearly expired.

At that surprising point, likely for both teams, Bill Goodman, who had since returned to his left halfback position on the field, suddenly exploded through the interior of the opposing line, which was still outfitted in "red and dark blue," at least sort of, anyway, and which, at that point in the game, had been required to deal with far too many explosions like that and for far too much of the game. And with both of his impressive guards running interference for him, the very capable Mr. Goodman managed to "clear," as they often say in the game, most of the "bearish secondary," before any of the members thereof fully realized what had just transpired, likely because of exhaustion at that point in the game. And with little effort thereafter, or, at least, not to any great extent, he continued on his "merry way," as it has often been said in classic literature, although largely about other related things, in a twenty six yard romp, virtually untouched, straight down the field, or relatively so, finally crossing the goal line, containing, by the way, the same, decorative, "dark blue and red colors."

That touchdown, as implied, was clearly a surprise to everyone, on and off the field, because both teams, at that point in the game, were visibly exhausted, "game weary," if you don't mind an old, overly worn, football expression. And, moreover, one would have normally expected that a team from a much larger high school in a far more prestigious conference, like the Western Conference, would likely "wear down," as they like to say in such uneven circumstances, a non conference adversary from a much smaller high school, not unlike the one in this instance, by the end of a hard fought game like that one. That it did not happen in this instance, given those competitive disadvantages, or those dissimilar high school demographics, if you prefer to think of it in that way, may seem to be, or to have been, somewhat puzzling, maybe even to the confrontational protagonists, themselves, at the time.

With the benefit of hindsight, however, or, if you prefer, an historical perspective, what happened, by way of that puzzling touchdown, nearly at the end of that fray, by a non-conference adversary, from a distinctly smaller high school, that late in the game, was, essentially, no different from what had been taking place on the "field of play," in the three previous outings with three other adversaries, none of whom, by the way, had any reason to believe that they would become the losing team at the time. In fact, most of them had every reason to believe that the outcome in the game would have been quite different, arithmetically, if nothing else, given the historically associated mediocrity of a football team from a smaller high school in rural Clinton County, part of the challenging regions of Appalachia.

In this inexplicable instance, however, if not in those occurring prior thereto,"The Boys From Across The River" departed from that historically associated mediocrity, notwithstanding the size of their high school, or the location thereof, or, for that matter, the historic nature of their football program, or even the challenges occurred thereby. And in this inexplicable instance, they did so by a final score of "twenty to nothing," including, interestingly enough, an extra point, subsequently, kicked by Bill Goodman, following that last touchdown, proving him, thereby, to be more than a capable backup in that department for the ever reliable John Edward Englert.

Moreover, given that mediocrity, and its historical association with the "Purple and White," as well the exception in this instance, or prior thereto, in the previous three games, and the likely reasons therefor, there was, obviously, something different, something special, something indefinable, about "The Boys From Across The River." And although that quality may have been indefinable, or seemingly so, it became more than translatable on a football field that season, because there was, obviously, something incredible about what they had done, what they could do and what they would continue to do on a football field, any football field. And their capacity to play like that, in almost any circumstance, against almost any adversary, no matter whom it may happen to be, or have been, was not lost, at that point in the season, on almost everyone, on and off of a football field. It is also likely that "The Boys From Across The River" . . . who were no more than impoverished kids out of the mountainous regions of Appalachia and who decided to cross the West Branch of the Susquehanna River, in order to play football for the perennially, pathetic "Bobcats" of Lock Haven High School . . . were beginning to believe it, too!

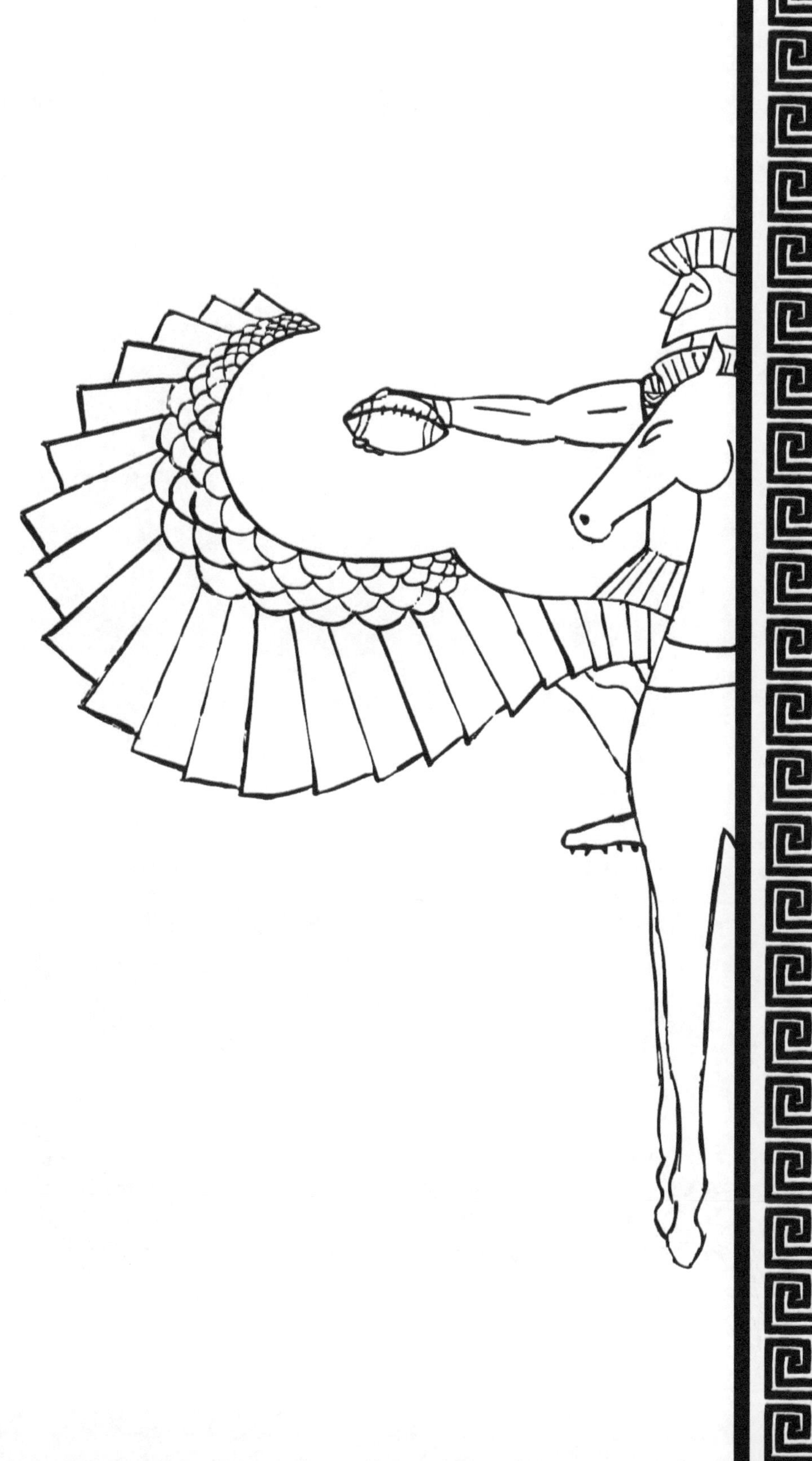

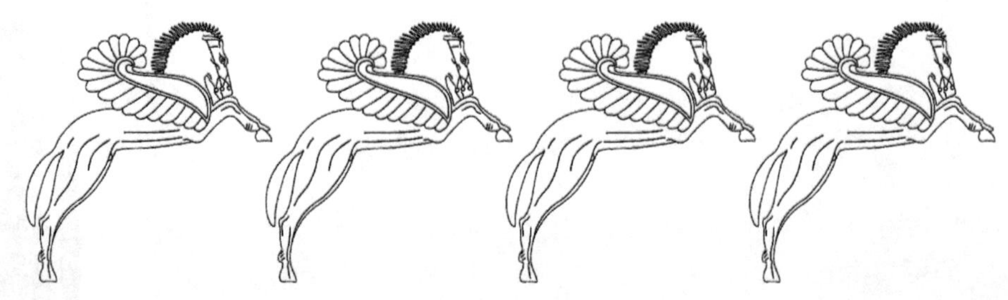

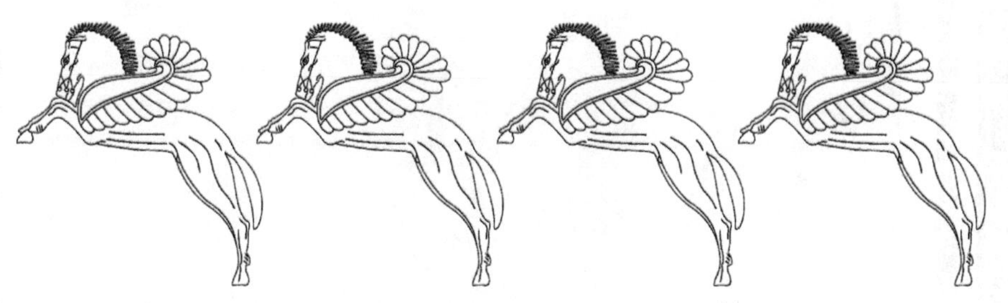

THE FIFTH GAME

IN THE FIFTH GAME OF THE SEASON, "THE BOYS FROM ACROSS THE RIVER" DEFEATED THE PERENNIALLY POWERFUL "PANTHERS" FROM LEWISTOWN HIGH SCHOOL, EVEN THOUGH THEY WERE ACTUALLY BEHIND AT THE END OF THE FIRST HALF, BECAUSE OF THEIR LEGENDARY PLAY IN THE SECOND HALF, WHICH, SEEMINGLY, DEFIED REALITY, NOT ONLY IN THAT INEXPLICABLE GAME, BUT IN THOSE OCCURRING PRIOR THERETO, ACCORDING TO THE FOLKLORE THAT WAS ARISING IN THOSE MOUNTAINOUS REGIONS.

UNFORTUNATELY, THE season included a visit to the J. Arlington Painter Stadium, on the following Friday evening, by the "Maroon and Steel" of the Lewistown High School "Panthers, from over in Mifflin County. I say, "unfortunately," because the "Bobcats," like nearly all of their counterparts in the Central States League, had some real difficulty in even playing, let alone in defeating, the, perennially powerful team from over the "Seven Mountains." This time, however, that historical problem, let alone the eventual outcome, involving a football game between the "Panthers" and the "Bobcats," seemed to devolve into irrelevance in the confrontation that was about to take place between those two teams on that auspicious occasion.

Indeed, the devolution began, following the opening kickoff, when "The Four Horsemen" surprised a traditionally "steely team," by, immediately, "marching down the field," in the language of the game, mostly in running plays, often in short yardage increments, by none other than Bill Goodman and Bob Crissman, playing at left and right halfback, respectively, the latter being a substitute on those occasions for "Chub" Schiavo, for no apparent reason. The "march," however, was also interrupted, on occasion, by a few, surprisingly successful, aerial displays to a highly visible Jan Bennet, over near the right and, subsequently, left sidelines, and, on rarer occasions, to a far less visible Wes Maggs, marooned in the middle of an adversarial secondary, if not in the midst of a totally surprised one!

It should be noted, at least at this point, that those, surprisingly, successful aerial displays were called upon by Dave Johnson, ever the astute quarterback, in order to keep the opposing secondary somewhat "honest," as it has been said in the game, because, prior thereto, they had begun to "crowd" the line of scrimmage, as it has often been said in those kind of circumstances, as a result of those consistently successful, short yardage, running-plays, covering, by that point in the game, over half of the football field.

When "The Four Horsemen" could, essentially, go no further, not in that foreign territory, following three unsuccessful efforts to do so, because of a resurgence of a line clad in "muddy steel," at the time, "Chub" Schiavo reentered the game, in order to carry the ball and the hopes of the hometown crowd on the fourth. And toward those challenging ends, he managed to scurry around the right side of a, formerly, obstinate, "steel-like" line, with two blockers, named Karch and Toner, leading the way. And upon, eventually, reaching a, partially, "open field," as they like to say in that kind of a situation, following their blocking assistance, of course, he began to outrun, or run around, everything that happened to be outfitted in "maroon and steel," now situated between him and the reason for being on the field, namely the goal line, twenty-one yards away.

It had been a long time, probably years, since anything in a "purple and white jersey" had visited that heavily guarded area, or, if you prefer the more traditional athletic reference, that heavily guarded end zone. And with John Englert, reliably, kicking an extra point, following that historical feat, "The Boys From Across The River" were now ahead of the dreaded and undefeated "Panthers," by "seven points," at least at that point in the game, which, in reality, was early in the first quarter.

Unfortunately, however, that football fact, not unlike most of those of a similar nature, historically associated with the "Maroon and Steel," would not continue, not for very much longer. No, the undefeated "Panthers," from across the "Seven Mountains," were not particularly happy about being on the short side of that score and in that game, even though it was no more than the first quarter of the game. And, significantly, they were a team with a lot of tradition, a lot of confidence and a lot of pride, which came from a lot of winning, over the years, even if they had to "come from behind," in the offensive language of the game, in order to do so, which, by the way, is exactly what they set out to do and in the second quarter, too!

It did not take them very long, either, because one of their defensive backs intercepted an errant pass, at his own forty-six yard line, shortly after the second quarter had begun. And following that unscripted-situation, he ran right past eleven, not one less, very surprised football players, with "purple and white not only on their uniforms," but on their embarrassed faces, too, stopping only when it was far too late to do anything about it, by anything with those kind of uncomfortably extended colors!

If the "bobcat bunch" had any illusion that, following their initial score, the game was going to become a proverbial, cake walk, not unlike most of their previous outings, that unfortunate bit of reality, in the nature of a surprising interception, likely changed their minds. And if it did not, the ability of that perennially unbeaten team, from across the "Seven Mountains," to, subsequently, mount a long drive down most of the field, ending with a score, shortly before the half had ended, certainly did! And because "The Boys From Across The River" were unable to return the favor, by a subsequent visit to the opposing end zone, not for the remainder of that disastrous period, which, of course, was the second period, they found themselves behind at the end of that half, for the very first time that season, by a "twelve to seven" score!

If the football game would have continued in the same manner in the second half, and if it would have, eventually, ended without any change in that score, it is not too difficult to realize what kind of an impact that would have upon a fast-growing legend. Apparently, however, that possibility was not lost on "The Boys From Across The River," because they became a different kind of football team that "kicked off," to commence the second half. And because of that difference, the, perennially undefeated team from across the "Seven Mountains" could not do much of anything to change their geography, not immediately thereafter, not in three wasted efforts. That was largely due to a resumption of the effective play by "The Seven Blocks of Granite," who had now become, virtually, immovable, or, if you will, legendary, once again!

Visibly shaken at that point, likely for that immovable reason, the newly humbled "Panthers" elected to punt on their fourth down, which, amazingly, traveled all the way down to the thirty one yard line of a resurrected-legend, which was an unbelievable punt, likely exceeding fifty one yards, especially for a high school senior, even one from across the "Seven Mountains." But, now, the real "unbelievable" was about to become part of the game or, at least, it was going to "begin to unfold," as they often say in those kinds of circumstances, even in athletic circumstances, such as football games. Because at that defining point, "The Boys From Across The River" had, apparently, decided that they had not come all of that legendary way to be mauled, once again, by a "Panther," not even one as formidable as the one now "dressed in maroon and steel," from across the "Seven Mountains."

For that reason, if not for the more legendary one, those unbelievable "Blocks of Granite," still "Seven" members strong," still in "Purple and White," at least sort of now, began to move their counterparts on the line of scrimmage down the field, in fairly large increments, too, over, nearly, the entire football field. And with "The Four Horsemen" dutifully following along, in a manner of speaking, from their advantageous positions in the backfield, that resurrected team, eventually, found themselves on the three yard line of a, seemingly, "crippled panther." And at that crucial point on the field, as well as in the game, itself, Bob Crissman, playing at right halfback, once again, for no apparent reason, easily crossed the goal line and into that, seemingly, hallowed territory, by merely following that legendary line, once again, which, in reality, was no more than an aggregation of "Seven" of "The Boys From Across The River."

Now the score had become a far more manageable "thirteen to twelve," if, of course, you happened to believe in legends, in a game in which everything had, obviously, become legendary, once again, notwithstanding the failure to kick an extra point by the normally automatic Mr. Englert. Nevertheless, automation and extra points aside, not to mention the failure thereof, it began to appear, at least at that point in the game, which, of course, was early in the third period, that "The Boys From Across The River," if you are still inclined to believe in legends, or, at least, miracles, may have become capable of driving the mighty "Panthers" back across the "Seven Mountains," to their home in Lewistown. And it may have even occurred to everyone on the field, or even off of it, for that matter, at least at that point in the game, that those, perennially, undefeated "Panthers," may no longer be the most formidable "cats on the field," nor even in the Central Counties League, not anymore!

If there had ever been any doubt about that transformation, taking place on the "field of play" at the time, it was certainly eliminated, shortly thereafter, by another "drive," which did not seem to be nearly as miraculous, given what had already transpired over the course of the game, by the efforts of those, indescribable, seven young men on the line of scrimmage. That "drive," mundane as it may have seemed, at least at that point in the game, if not at that point in the season, took place late in the third quarter. And the impact thereof forced a, perennially, undefeated football team "back on its heels," so to speak, not to mention back down the field, too, toward their own goal line, and with much less effort this time. Ending the "drive," or the competitive drama, which may be a far more accurate way of describing the situation, at least at that point in the game, "one" of "The Four Horsemen," starting nearly every game at left halfback, Bill Goodman, executed a "coup de grace," so to speak, by a three yard plunge into the end zone, a "maroon and steel end zone," poorly defended at that point, by a fairly exhausted defensive line, with the "steel" largely in absence. And with that, the score, in the absence of an extra point contribution by the newly humbled Mr. Englert, became "nineteen," for the resurrected, "Cats-from-Clinton County," and only "twelve," for their diminished "feline counterparts," from over the "Seven Mountains," in Mifflin County.

That was not the end of the onslaught, however, even though it was nearly the end of the fourth quarter and the end of the game, too. In fact, shortly before the game had ended, one of the discombobulated members of the "maroon and steel backfield," fumbled, after inadvertently, not to mention uncomfortably, running into a "Moose," following what seemed to be a rather nice twelve yard gain, at least at that point in a rapidly diminishing contest. And following that "bone crushing collision," as they are apt to say in the game, the "Moose," formerly in a "purple and white uniform," which, now, more closely resembled the turf, from which he sprang, alertly picked up the loose ball, almost immediately thereafter. Spinning around now, within minutes thereafter, he began to retrace his steps, through a thoroughly disoriented and dispirited "maroon and steel team," with, surprisingly, little trouble, given the competitive nature of that, formerly, undefeated football team. And following thirty nine yards of what could only be described as a rather ponderous-gallop, through a, virtually, unobstructed football field, he, finally, ended up in their end zone, the "maroon and steel end zone," which, at that point, was beginning to look more like a way-station, open to the public, or, at least, that part of it that comprised, "The Boys From Across The River."

It would prove to be the last score by the 'Purple and White," in a rather unpredictable game, historically so, if nothing else, because, among other inexplicable things, which have already been recounted, and in some detail, too, John Englert's extra point kick was blocked, once again, leaving the score for the home team at "twenty-five," even though the last quarter, in a four-quarter football game, had not yet come to an end.

Actually, however, the game had, in fact, come to an end for the "purple and white varsity," because their Coach decided, at that point in the game, that it had become "so far out of reach," in the language of the game, by anything emanating out of Mifflin County, that he decided not to embarrass the "maroon and steel visitors," any further, by finishing the game with his varsity still on the field. Realizing that opportune fact, almost before it had become one, a reinvigorated "maroon marauder," still of the varsity kind, managed to score, rather quickly and without too much difficulty, on the "purple and white junior varsity," in the waning moments of that quarter, the last quarter of that football game. And by doing so, they, thereby, increased their score by another "six points," to give that "maroon and steel team" a total of "nineteen points," for the game, which, of course, was

still short of the "twenty five points," scored by "The Boys From Across The River."

Need I remind you, however, that the recent "maroon and steel score," which, of course, was their final score, and which was the last accomplishment of their under-performing varsity, likely occurred because "The Four Horsemen" and "The Seven Blocks of Granite" had been retired from the game by an overly sympathetic Coach, who, subsequently, replaced them with the junior varsity for the remainder of the game. Thereafter, both of those varsity units spent the remainder of the game on their "bench," so to speak, congratulating each other because of what they had just historically accomplished . . . with respect to Counties and Mountains and Schools and Mascots and Colors, or, more specifically, "The Mifflin County" and "The Seven Mountains" and "The Lewistown High School" and "The "Panthers" and "The Maroon and Steel!"

The conversation, if we may call it that, took place amidst a great amount of oversized language and boisterous laughter, by every member of that excited varsity, except, possibly, Dave Johnson, their acknowledged leader, on and off the football field, whose composure was never anything less than restrained, in almost any circumstance, not excluding being on the verge of an historic victory over a, perennially, powerful team of "Panthers," in "Maroon and Steel," and playing for the Lewistown High School, located, across the "Seven Mountains," in Mifflin County.

It would turn out to be, in looking back now, the closest that anything in a football uniform would ever come to actually dispel a fast-growing legend, which would appear, weekly, that season on a high school gridiron, in one town or another, in central Pennsylvania. In fact, in looking back once again, it would turn out to be the only loss suffered that season by a, perennially, powerful football team, in "maroon and steel," from the town of Lewistown, just across the "Seven Mountains," in Mifflin County, Pennsylvania. That fact, or, rather, those facts, were not lost on the folklore that was rapidly gaining traction throughout that mountainous region about the legendary play, over five games, by a group of young boys known, at the time, as "The Boys From Across The River," who remained unbeaten and untied at that point in the season, notwithstanding the caliber of their opposition in most of those games!

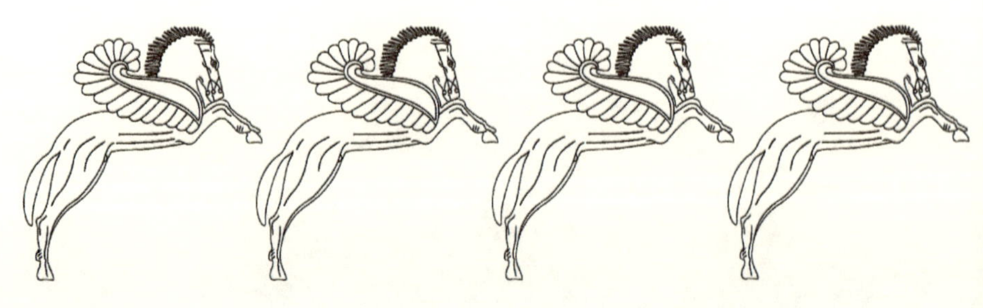

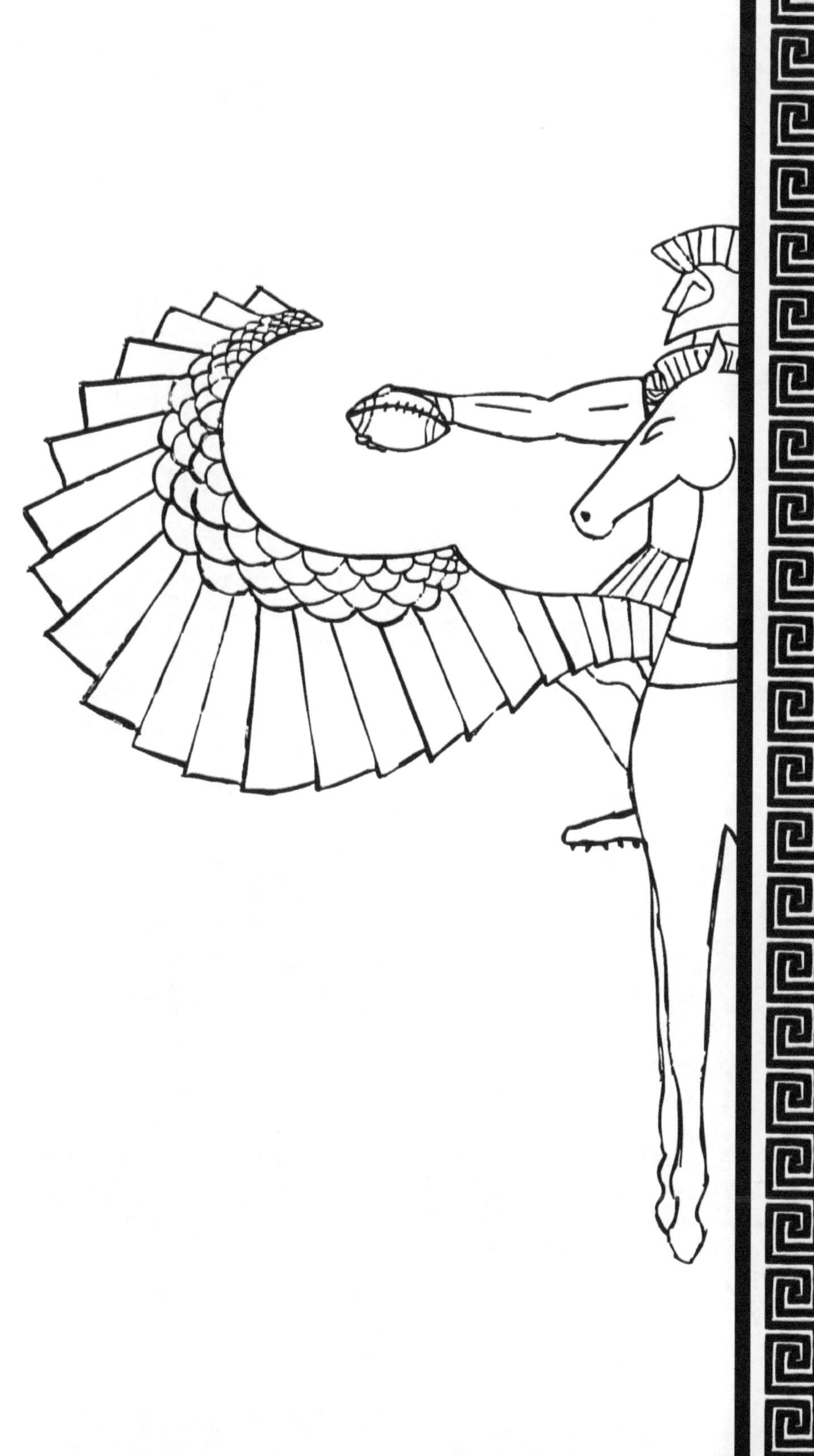

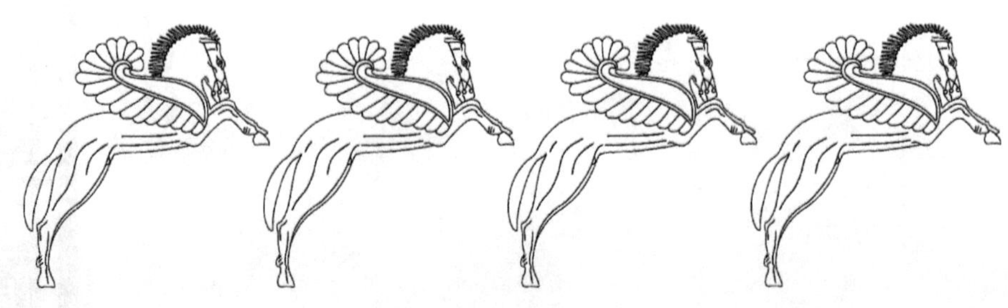

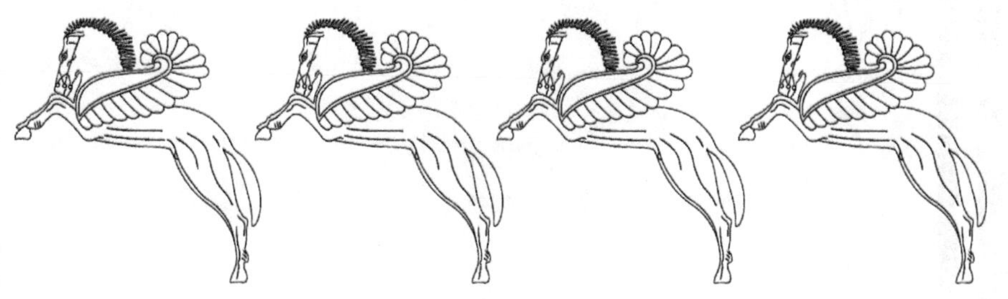

THE SIXTH GAME

"THE BOYS FROM ACROSS THE RIVER" DEFEATED THE "ORANGE AND BLACK" OF THE MILTON HIGH SCHOOL "PANTHERS," IN GAME SIX OF THAT SEASON, BY THE UNSEEMLY SCORE OF "TWENTY SEVEN TO NOTHING," LARGELY AS A RESULT OF A CONTINUATION OF THE LEGENDARY PLAY BY THE "SEVEN BLOCKS OF GRANITE" AND "THE FOUR HORSEMEN," IN THE OPINION OF THE FOLKLORE THAT HAD, SUBSEQUENTLY, BECOME PERVASIVE THROUGHOUT THAT MOUNTAINOUS REGION.

The following week, that growing legend confronted another "Panther," on another Friday evening, but outfitted, in that instance, in the "Orange and Black" of Milton High School, over in Northumberland County. And if those "orange and black looking pussycats" did not believe in legends at the beginning of that affair, after a "twenty seven to nothing" shellacking by one "outfitted in purple and white," called the "Bobcats," they certainly did by the end of that game. And with that score in mind, if not the reasons therefor, there really was not much that one could say about a team that was beaten that badly in a football game that took place in their very own stadium as well. In fact, they really could not do much of anything on the field, not offensively, not during any one of those four quarters, not of any consequence, anyway, other than, possibly, punt the ball on a fourth down, following a disastrous attempt to run or pass on the previous three. They couldn't even score on the "purple and white junior varsity," who, essentially, were not part of the legend, but who played as though they were and for most of the second half, too!

Meanwhile, some of the legend-makers in the backfield, or, if you will, "The Four Horsemen," ran all over the place, the other team's place, that is, for almost the entire four quarters of the game. In fact, they scored on Bill Goodman's eleven yard run in the first quarter; John Englert's twenty two yard run in the first quarter; Dave Johnson's forty eight yard run in the second quarter; and, even, Kenny Miller's seven yard run in the fourth quarter, when most of the varsity had been replaced by the junior varsity on the "field of play." And you should not be surprised to learn, certainly not by this point, that John Englert made three of his four attempts at kicking an extra point. That he actually failed at kicking one of them, because the football hit the crossbar and bounced away, did not seem to do anything to dispel a fast-growing legend about a high school football team that season, which, among a number of other remarkable things, seemed to automatically score extra points by kicking them!

With that in mind, if not everything else that occurred during the course of that game, as a result of the incredible play, once again, by "The Boys From Across The River," it is probably safe to say, if something should be said about such a one-sided affair, that the "Panthers" returned to Milton with their tail between their "black and orange wobbly legs," because the final score became, as I have already indicated, "twenty-seven" for the victorious and vainglorious football team from Lock Haven High School, and "absolutely nothing," for the defeated and deflated football team from Milton High School.

Following the inability of Milton High School to even score on "The Boys From Across The River," which, of course, was not the first time that this had happened over the course of the season, the folklore now pervasive in that mountainous region suggested that nothing in the region was capable of standing in the way of the legendary play associated with that unbeaten and untied football team, maybe nothing in the State, itself! Certainly, it had not been any of the high school football teams that had already gone down in defeat, prior to that point in the season, as a result of the legendary play of "The Boys From Across The River."

Nevertheless, a disbelieving journalist, from, nearby, Lycoming County, pointed out that the high schools in some of the towns and cities remaining on the schedule for that football season were far larger, with far more impressive football programs, than the one in Lock Haven! And, what's more, he could not remember any of the football teams from those kind of impressive high schools ever losing a game to a team from a smaller and more rural high school, with a more challenging football program associated therewith, like the one in Lock Haven. In fact, with respect to one of those schools, the large high school in the City of Williamsport, in Lycoming County, Pennsylvania, called the "Millionaires," no less, he could not remember them losing a game at all, not over the last several years, anyway, and, certainly, not to a football team from a smaller high school like the one in Lock Haven, in, nearby, Clinton County, Pennsylvania.

There appeared to be an implicit rejoinder in that pervasive folklore, however, if you could really call it a rejoinder, which seemed to acknowledge the logic borne out of all of that history with respect to all of those impressive football programs associated with all of those larger high schools, but which seemed to answer, by reminding the logicians and the historians, if not that doubting journalist, that none of those football teams from those larger and more impressive high schools have ever faced a football team widely known as "The Boys From Across The River." And whatever that may mean, which is, admittedly, hard to explain, the fact is that it probably explains everything!

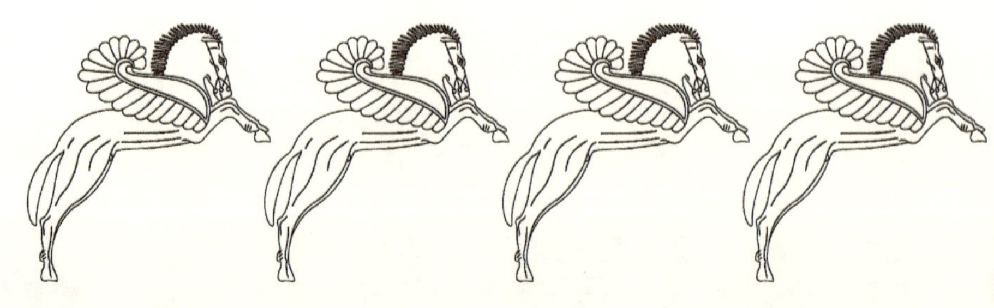

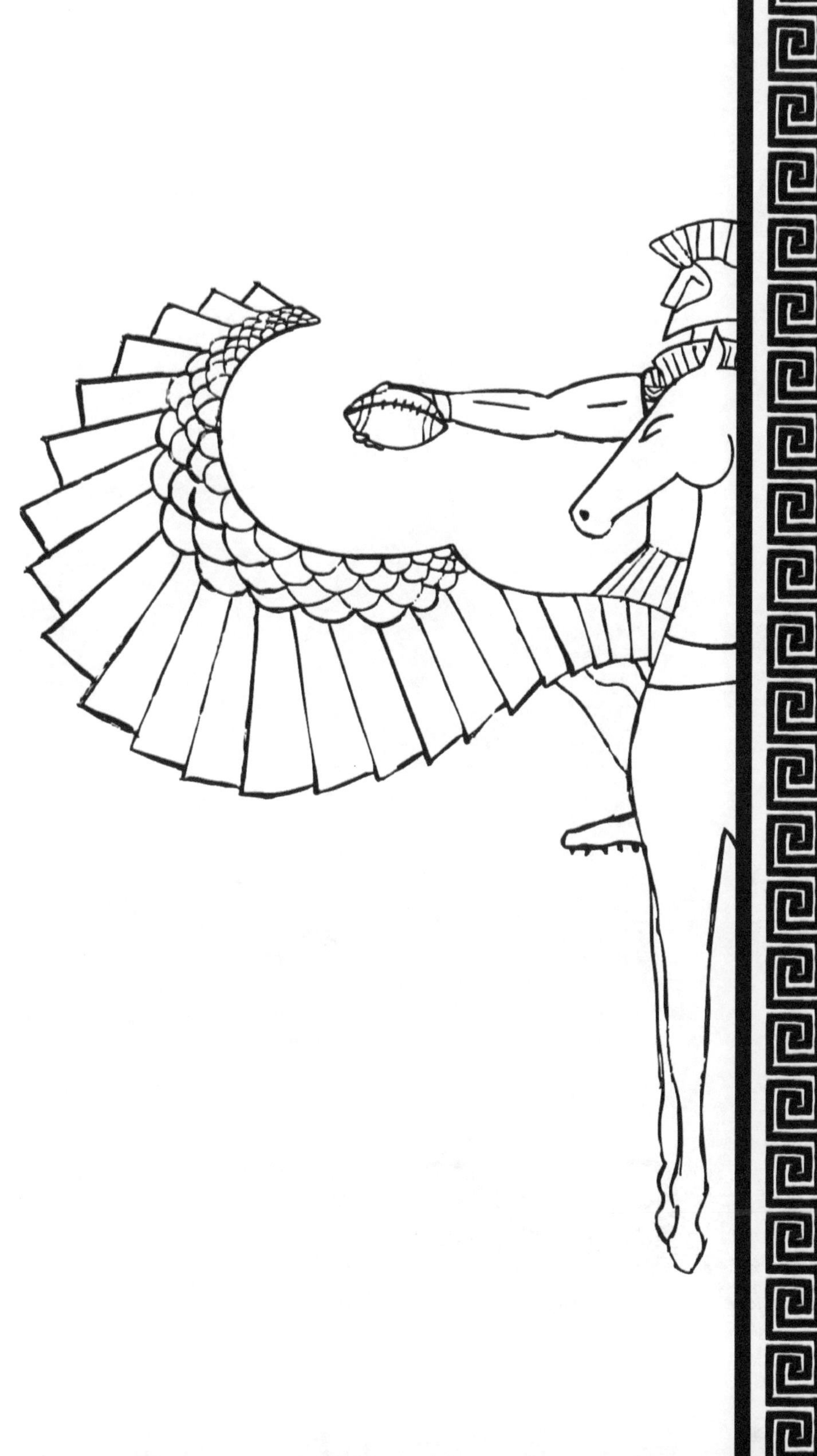

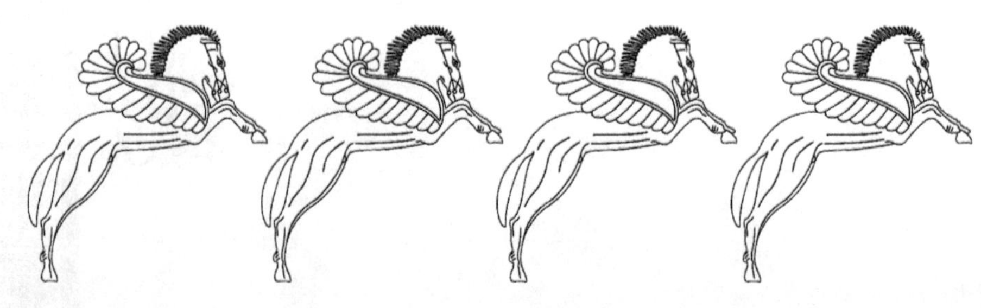

THE SEVENTH GAME

THE VICTORY OVER THE "MOUNTIES" FROM SOUTH WILLIAMSPORT HIGH SCHOOL, IN THE SEVENTH GAME OF THAT SEASON, BECAME MORE THAN LEGENDARY IN THE FOLKLORE THAT HAD BEEN ARISING IN THOSE MOUNTAINOUS REGIONS, NOT ONLY BECAUSE OF THE VICTORY, ITSELF, OR BECAUSE THE TEAM WAS UNBEATEN AND UNTIED AT THAT POINT IN THE SEASON, BUT BECAUSE OF THE NATURE OF A FOOTBALL TEAM THAT SEEMED TO HAVE BECOME AS UNREAL IN THAT GAME AS IT WAS IN THE SIX GAMES PRECEDING IT. AND THAT IS NOT EXCLUDING A NUMBER OF OTHER REAL THINGS, ASSOCIATED THEREWITH, NOT EXCLUDING AN "AGELESS CHANT," A "PECULIAR MARCHING BAND," LED BY "MAJORETTES IN GHOST-LIKE WHITE ATTIRE," THE "SEVEN, ALWAYS SEVEN, CHEERLEADERS," A "TIMELESS FIGHT SONG," AND, WHAT'S MORE, A FOOTBALL TEAM CALLED, INCREDIBLY, "THE BOYS FROM ACROSS THE RIVER."

One week later, the "Mounties," camped out in South Williamsport High School, in, nearby, Lycoming County, rode down the Susquehanna Valley on their "blue and white steeds," or was it really in their "blue and white jerseys," for a football game against a growing legend, about an unbeaten and untied football team, in the J. Arlington Painter Stadium, which was located, almost magically, if not mythically, at the juncture of Fourth and Spring Streets in Lock Haven, Pennsylvania.

The magic, if not the myth, arose from the significance of that address, which, of course, was the address of that Stadium, but which, actually, transcended, in significance, the location of the Stadium, because it was also on one side of a lengthy and tall no-longer-existing bridge, spanning a number of railroad tracks, far down below it, known at the time as, simply, the "Overhead Bridge." And the "Overhead Bridge," effectively, if not remarkably, connected the Stadium, on one side of it, to the "Lock Haven High School," on the other side of it, where "The Boys" were students at the time. Moreover, of even more consequence, especially with respect to this story, that is where they changed into their football uniforms, down in the basement locker room, before leaving the school, just before a game and commencing, thereafter, to climb the lengthy stairs to the "Overhead Bridge" and beginning the long trip across, on their way to play another football team, in another high school game, on another Friday evening, in the J. Arlington Painter Stadium.

Not surprisingly, nearly everyone seated in that "Stadium," on a Friday evening, knew, from years of experience, that "The Boys" would begin to rumble across that "Overhead Bridge" as soon as the "Seven Cheerleaders" would begin their "Ageless Chant," which, remarkably, would always occur at exactly eight o'clock in the evening, not a minute before or after, and which, invariably, would begin, "two bits, four bits, six bits, a Dollar, Everyone for Lock Haven, Stand-Up and Holler!"

At that point, at that very point, which, of course, was at the conclusion thereof, "The Boys From Across The River," which is what they were called at the time, would begin to appear, almost magically, if not mythically, up there, on that "Overhead Bridge," in full uniform, no less, including cleats and helmets, on their way, not simply across, but on their way toward becoming a legend, if not the subject of folklore, subsequent thereto, arising everywhere in that mountainous area, and, possibly, even a myth, everywhere else, years later, in this great nation!

Meanwhile, upon the appearance of "The Boys," up there, on that "Overhead Bridge," rumbling along in their brightly colored, "purple and white uniforms," nearly everyone in the Stadium would, now, stand-up and begin to cheer! At about the same time, the "Marching Band," would, automatically, strike-up the "Timeless Fight Song," which has, always, begun: "Purple and White, it's up to you to win This Fight; our Gallant Sons will Ever Strive for Victory . . ." And which the "Seven," always seven, "Cheerleaders" would now, typically, begin to sing, along with nearly everyone else, too, who were now standing on their feet, in that, now, rocking Stadium!

It would not stop, either, not any of it, not until all eleven of those "Boys" had descended the lengthy stairs from that "Overhead Bridge;" and they had begun to find their way into the Stadium. At that point, everything would seem to subside, somewhat, but when the last player finally entered the stadium and joined the others, up near midfield, where they were briefly throwing around a couple of footballs, it would prompt a deafening roar, all over again, from the hometown crowd, who were still on their feet, cheering and stomping, all at the same time!

The whole scenario . . . including the magical time of occurrence, which, of course, was at eight o'clock in the evening, exactly on the hour, following that "Ageless Chant" by the "Seven," always seven, "Cheerleaders" . . . did nothing to dispel what was fast becoming something out of another world, something unreal, if not distinctly surreal, not simply in legendary terms on the field, but, subsequently, folklore off of it, everywhere in those mountainous communities, and, eventually, with discussion and disbelief, mythical, years later, nearly everywhere in the State of Pennsylvania, if not in the Nation, itself.

Well, "Chants" and "Cheerleaders" and "Marching Bands" and "Fight Songs," not to mention "Overhead Bridges," were, apparently, not about to stop the, unimpressed, "Blue and White," who had already arrived at the J. Arlington Painter Stadium, in order confront a legend, with mythical implications, too, especially on the line of scrimmage, if not on that "Overhead Bridge."

Indeed, the "Mounties" were well aware of those legendary stories, by that point in the season, not to mention the futile efforts of their predecessors to "run the ball," as they say in the game, on those "Seven Blocks of Legend." And in order to avoid the consequences of those preceding, if not futile, efforts, in prior games that season, an, extraordinarily, talented quarterback for the "Blue and White," who would go on to play for the Maize and Blue of the University of Michigan, a few years later, passed and passed again, and, then, again, for short and, even, longer, yardage, as the occasion permitted or even required, until his team, eventually, reached the twenty seven yard line, belonging to a completely bewildered legend, certainly at that point in the game. Then, in order to change things up a little bit, all of them mounted their horses once again, and as "Mounties," proceeded to run over, around and through, a thoroughly disoriented defensive line, legendary or not, for an inevitable, if not surprising, touchdown, early in the first quarter. And if all of that had not been surprising enough, they also ran for the extra point, too; quite successfully, I might add!

The second quarter could best be described by an inability on the part of the "Mounties," now with a "seven to nothing" lead, to mount any form of a running game, not anymore, likely as a result of a reorientation, if not a rejuvenation of "The Seven Blocks of Granite." And, consequently, a belated, but fortunate, return to their legendary play, or their legendary ways, whichever alternative you deem to be more appropriate at that point in the game, if not at that point in the season. And the few aerial attempts, occurring in between some of those ruinous runs, were equally unsuccessful, largely because of having lost, at least at that point in the game, their surprising nature.

Meanwhile, an, inexplicably, ineffective offense, in both of those two quarters, if you could even describe it as that, conducted by nothing that even resembled "The Four Horsemen," not in their previous outings, anyway, would, periodically, "drive down the field," as they say in the game, to the, so-called, "red-zone" of their "mounted adversary," defined, for your athletic edification, by the proximity to the goal line. At that promising point, however, they were continually thwarted, either by a fumble, or by an intercepted pass, or by a broken play, or by some other miscalculation, from, eventually, scoring. Consequently, "The Boys From Across The River," if you still wanted to call them that, left the "field of play," in the language of the game, at the end of that half, the first half of that football game, without a score, not to mention with a legend that was in serious tatters at that point, because that mounted team was now ahead of them by "seven points."

In the second half, however, everything changed, dramatically, by the way, by becoming far more consistent with the previous games that season, largely as a result of a continuation of the legendary play, on "both sides of the ball," so to speak, by "The Boys From Across The River." As a result, nothing in a "blue and white jersey," mounted or otherwise, could, effectively, do much of anything, or, essentially, go anywhere, by any means whatsoever, largely as a result of the legendary play, once again, of "The Seven Blocks of Granite." And, moreover, John Englert and Dave Johnson, "Two" of "The Four Horsemen," must have realized that the game, if not the legend, was in serious jeopardy, so, in a manner of speaking, they decided to eliminate the threat, by their offensive performance over the remainder of that closely contested football game!

Overhead railroad bridge at Fourth Street, Lock Haven, PA, February 1989. Photographed by Jack Frey.

In the case of Dave Johnson, it occurred by way of a quarterback draw as well as a subsequent broken pass play, in which he raced, in each one of those instances, for over half of the football field, for a, virtually, unimpeded score, in the early and latter part of the third quarter. Not to be outdone by his lifelong friend, from across the river, too, John Englert, in his inimical fashion, bulldozed his way through the opposing line, athletically speaking, and into their well-traveled end zone, at least by that point in the game, for a four yard touchdown, with a little less than half of that "mounted team" trying to hang onto him at one point or another!

Subsequently, ridding himself of most of that "blue and white baggage," following his inartful touchdown, with some assistance, by the way, from both of the referees, a taciturn Mr. Englert returned to the field, in order to kick an extra point, which he subsequently did. The absence of a similar success with respect to the earlier two scores by the "Purple and White," in that half, the second half of that football game, can, apparently, be ascribed to the less artful kicking foot of Mr. Goodman. On the other hand, it should be noted that John Englert's kicking consistency, over all seven games at that point in the season, began to qualify that dependable foot, if not the player to whom it belonged, for something beyond legendary consideration, possibly even reaching folklore, itself, if not mythology, years later.

In any event, as you can easily see, the game did not end as it had begun, because "The Boys From Across The River," eventually, "went home," in a manner of speaking, with another victory, although it may not have been their most impressive one, by a "nineteen to seven" score, which, when you look back at their season at that point, was the seventh one in a row. And if nothing else, that number, given the nature of some of the competition, appears to have succeeded in making that accumulation legendary on the field, if not folklore, off of it, and, following a great amount of discussion and disbelief, thereafter, possibly even mythical, years later.

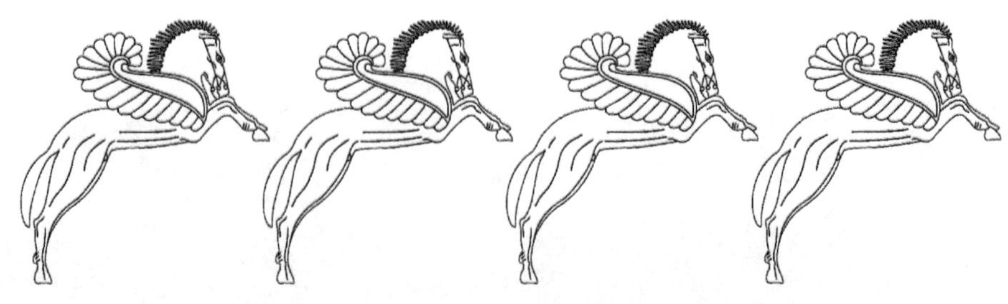

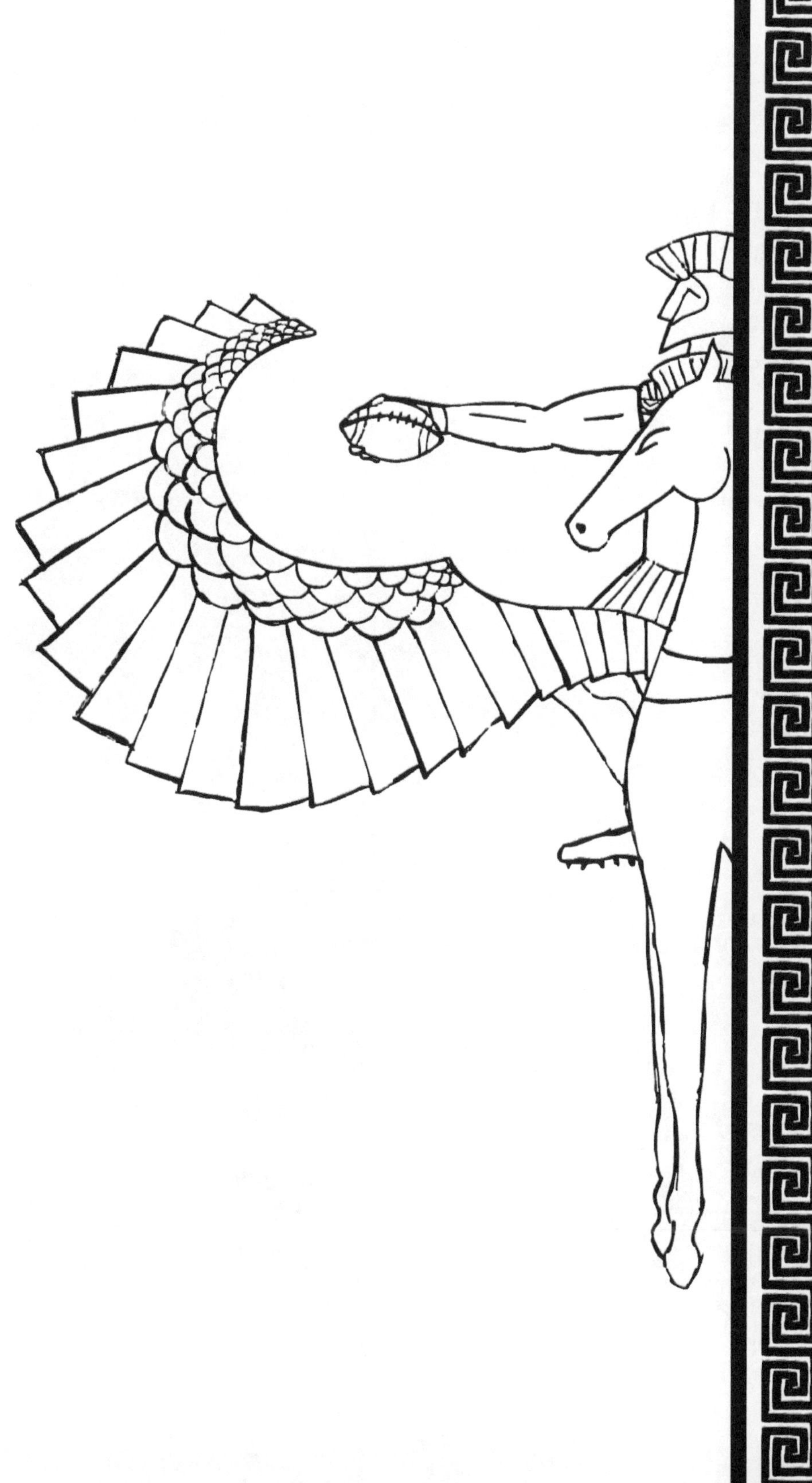

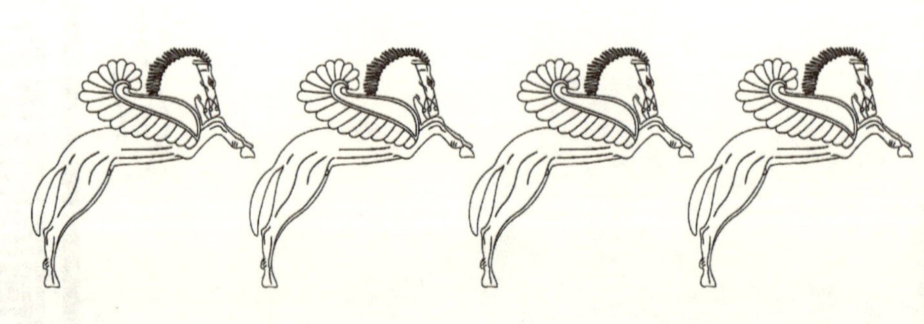

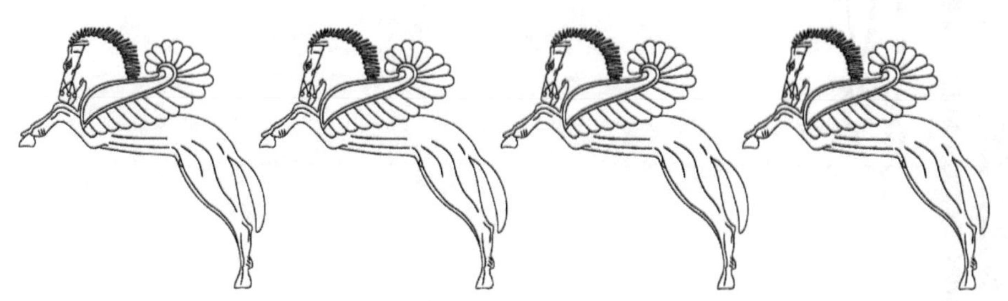

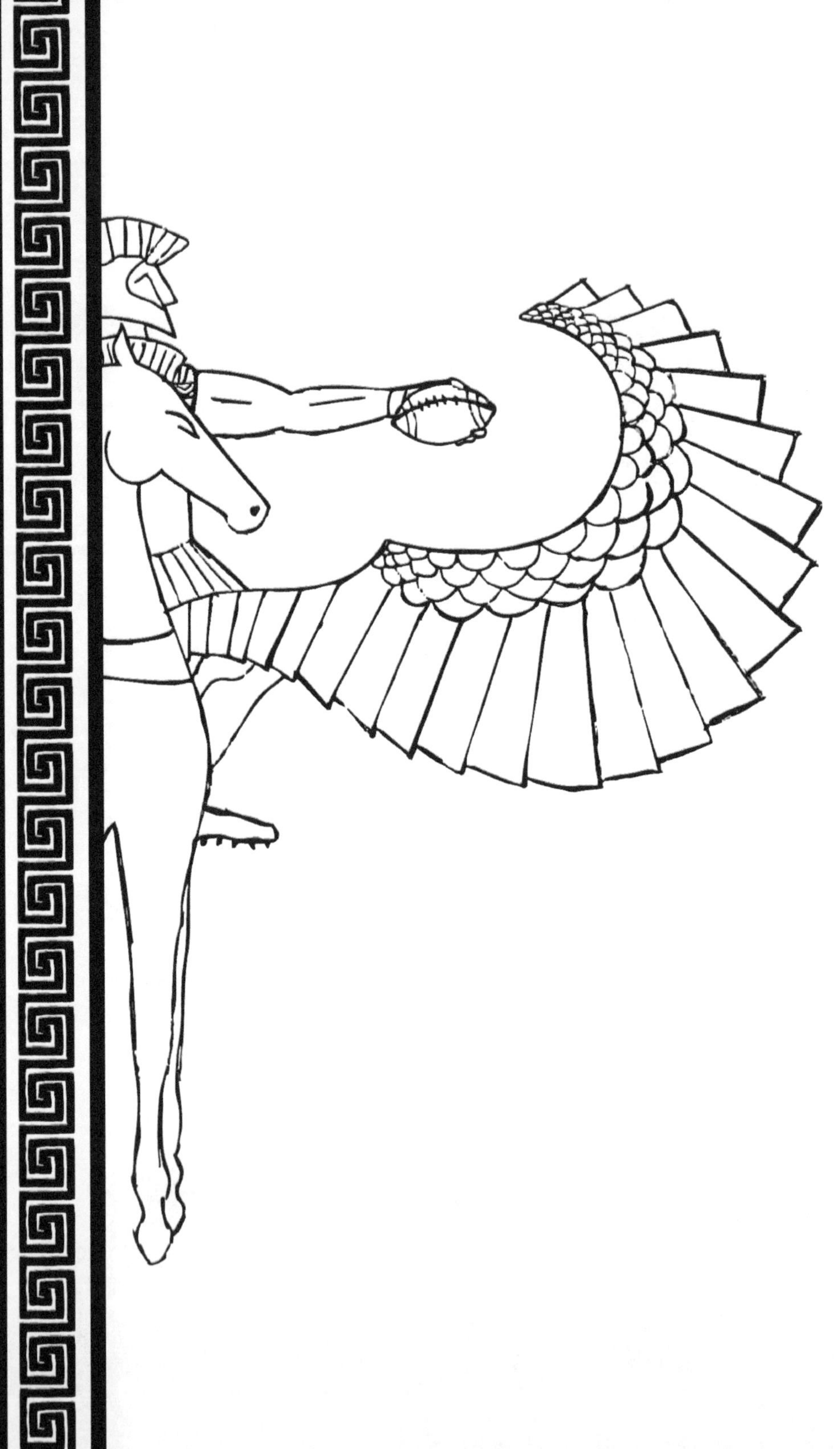

THE EIGHTH GAME

HAVING DESTROYED THE "GOLDEN EAGLES" OF TYRONE HIGH SCHOOL, IN THE EIGHTH GAME OF THE SEASON, BY THE SCORE OF "TWENTY SIX TO NOTHING," ON A SNOW COVERED-FIELD, NO LESS, THE ABILITY OF "THE FOUR HORSEMEN" TO "MOVE THE BALL," AS THEY SAY IN THE GAME, IN THOSE KIND OF CIRCUMSTANCES, WHILE THE "GOLDEN EAGLES," COULD NOT, SEEMED TO SUGGEST TO ONE JOURNALIST THAT "THE FOUR HORSEMEN," ACTUALLY, HAD "WINGS ON THEIR FEET," NOT UNLIKE THEIR MYTHICAL COUNTERPARTS, HERMES AND MERCURY; OR, IN THE ALTERNATIVE, IT MAY HAVE, ACTUALLY, SUGGESTED, IN THE ABSENCE OF SUCH HYPERBOLIC JOURNALISTIC SPECULATIONS, THAT THE CONSISTENCY OF THEIR LEGENDARY PLAY THAT SEASON, NO MATTER IN WHAT KIND OF A CIRCUMSTANCE OR WITH WHAT KIND OF AN OPPONENT, IS AN INDICATION THAT "THE BOYS FROM ACROSS THE RIVER" MAY HAVE, ACTUALLY, TRANSCENDED THOSE CIRCUMSTANCES, OR THOSE OPPONENTS, OR THOSE GAMES, OR THOSE FRIDAY EVENINGS, OR EVEN TIME, ITSELF.

The following week, an undefeated and untied football team, accompanied by a fast-growing legend, traveled, southwesterly, down the Bald Eagle Valley into Blair County, in order to confront a, twice-defeated, Tyrone Football Team, wearing the "Orange and Black" of a "Golden Eagle." And that "orange and black team" was more than prepared to ignore the legend, growing over those previous seven weeks, and inflict the first loss of the season upon the legend-makers from Clinton County.

Unfortunately, however, they had to do it in a blinding snowstorm, unseasonably so, sweeping down out of the surrounding mountain sides, throughout the entire game, which seemed to impede their effort, somewhat, if nothing else did. In fact, as a rather awkward bird on the ground, by nature, that "golden eagle" was not able to "run the ball," not very well, anyway, especially not in those snowy conditions, no matter which member of its "bird-like backfield" was giving it a try. What's more, it could not easily take flight, either, not in those snowy conditions, and that is not even to mention the trouble caused by that legendary line and that impenetrable secondary, both of which began that game wearing the "Purple and White" of Lock Haven High School.

To illustrate those, unbelievably, snowy conditions, throughout the entire game, I have enclosed, below, a photograph thereof, taken during the course of that challenging game, at least for the "Golden Eagles.

In the end, the "hapless eagles," were reduced to defending their "feathery-football field" from an onslaught, carried out by "The Four Horsemen," clad now in a barely visible white, the purple having vanished some time ago in those, unbelievably, snowy conditions on the field. And on top of being virtually invisible, in a white-out sort of situation, they seemed, during the course of the game, to have developed "wings on their feet," according to an imaginative journalist, who was reporting on the snowy situation on the following day, which, in his subsequent opinion, was not unlike their mythical and classical counterparts, "Hermes and Mercury."

Indeed, with those apparent "wings," Bill Goodman, still playing at left halfback, seemed to soar over eleven mired-down, "eagle like adversaries," or, if you will, "grounded golden birds," according to the same imaginative journalist, in a thirty four yard, virtually invisible,

touchdown flight; or if you are less inclined to believe in journalistic or mythical conclusions, classical or otherwise, a comparable sliding and slippery score by a snowy ghost, either one of which took place, of course, in the first quarter of that game. And, subsequent thereto, he managed a, virtually, invisible sixty six yard flight to "pay-dirt," according to the same journalist; or if you haven't changed your unimaginative mind, a comparable sliding and slippery score, in the, virtually, knee-high snow, either one of which took place, of course, in the second quarter.

Compounding those unbelievable, or, nearly, invisible, aerial achievements, or, if you will, what may have actually occurred, in the absence of mythology or journalism, that is, John Englert followed suit, in the third period, with a lengthy flight of his own in that blinding snowstorm, or so it seemed, once again, to that imaginative journalist, landing, as it were, in the "eagle's nest," once again, or, if you will, their partially obscured end zone. And to satisfy your understandable curiosity, or, more likely, disbelief, at least at this point in the story, it was, actually, impossible to ascertain, at the time, whether any of those flights were metaphoric or literal, earth-bound or not, because of the challenging

conditions in both of those spheres, according to the same, now more realistic, journalist, this time.

Well, whatever may have been the case, Wes Maggs, still playing at right end, concluded that "unbelievable scoring," in a barely visible game, by catching an eleven yard pass of what appeared to be a ball-of-ice, otherwise known, in far more favorable conditions, as a football. And the area in which that icy-ball landed, in his partially frozen hands, was, purportedly, a snow filled end zone, belonging to a team of "flightless eagles," formerly golden in color, who, by the way, seemed to be frozen in place at the time, if not for all time, according to the same, now ambivalent, journalist.

I should also note that, following two of those invisible, if not unbelievable, scores, Bill Goodman was called upon to kick the frozen footballs into the snowy air, which he did, and which, ultimately, became lost in a white oblivion, but which were, nevertheless, counted as extra points by the game officials, largely because they could not see well enough to conclude otherwise, in the opinion of the same, now more speculative, journalist. Surprisingly, John Englert remained on the "bench," during that extra point time, because his kicking toe was suffering from frostbite, which was obviously the explanation for his failure to convert on the two extra point efforts that preceded Mr. Goodman's subsequent two invisible successes!

With the addition of those two extra points, I will tenuously conclude that the "Orange and Black," at least at the beginning of that game, "Golden Eagles," who suffered from a significant amount discoloration, if not disorientation, by the end of that snowy-affair, were rather soundly beaten, by the score of "twenty-six to nothing," ostensively by an undefeated and untied football team. In reality, however, it may have, actually, been by a "blinding snowstorm," sweeping down out of the surrounding mountain sides at an unseasonable time of the year; or, possibly, it may have been, according to the same imaginative journalist, the purported, "winged feet," on "The Four Horsemen!"

With the latter in mind, if not their, purported, soaring, scoring methodology, I ask you, as I have myself, for decades now, whether we are actually dealing with something beyond "winged feet," or a "blinding snowstorm," and which may not have been limited by that kind of a phenomena, or those kind of circumstances, or even by time, itself; or to put the question somewhat differently, has the occurrence of that kind of legendary play by "The Boys From Across The River," in any kind of circumstance, involving any kind of opposition, gone on to transcend folklore, at some point in time, and, become, from our historical perspective, mythical in the end?!

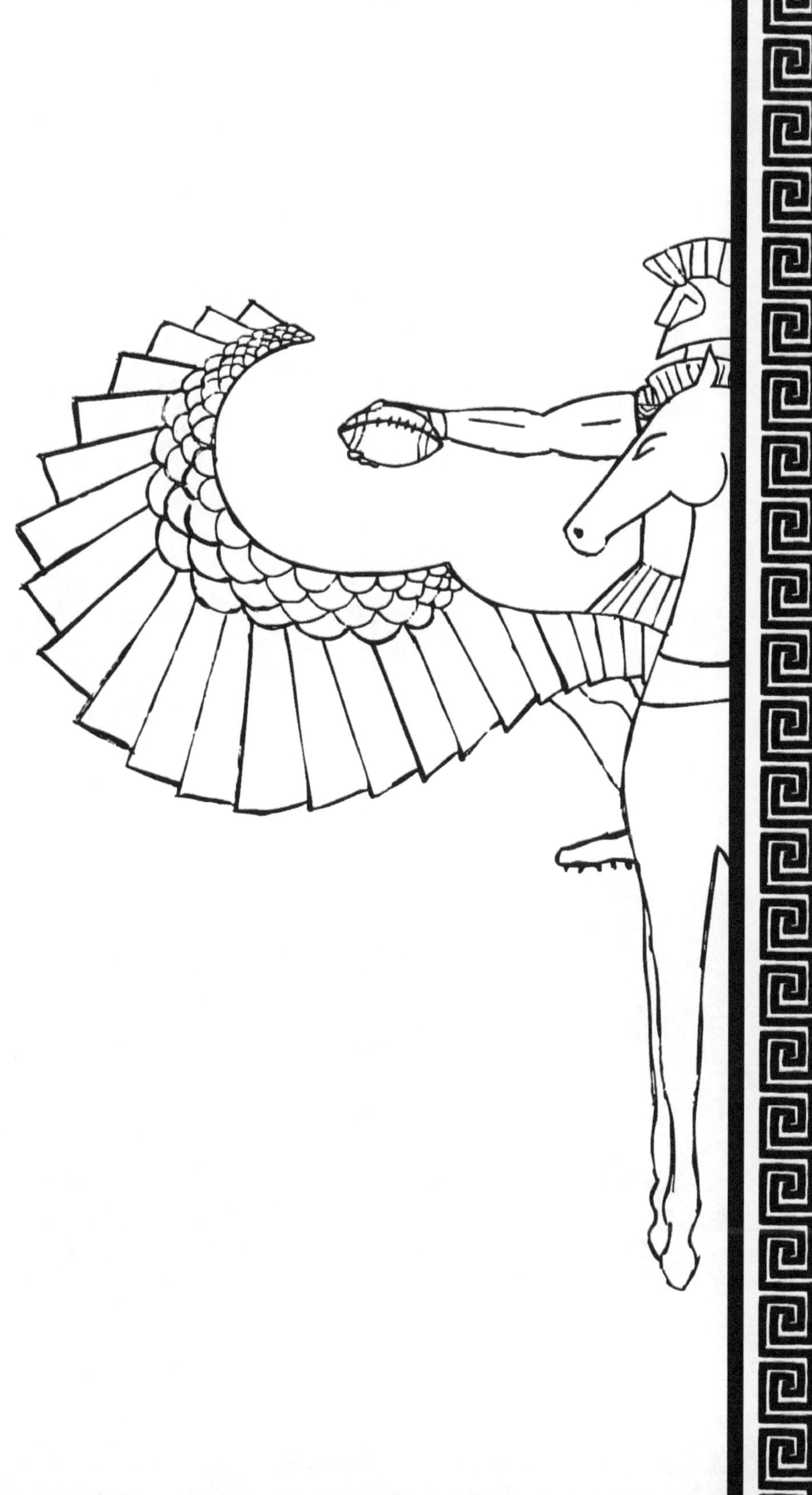

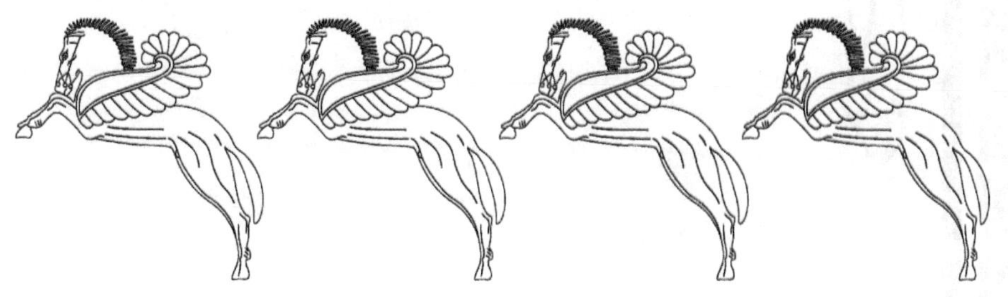

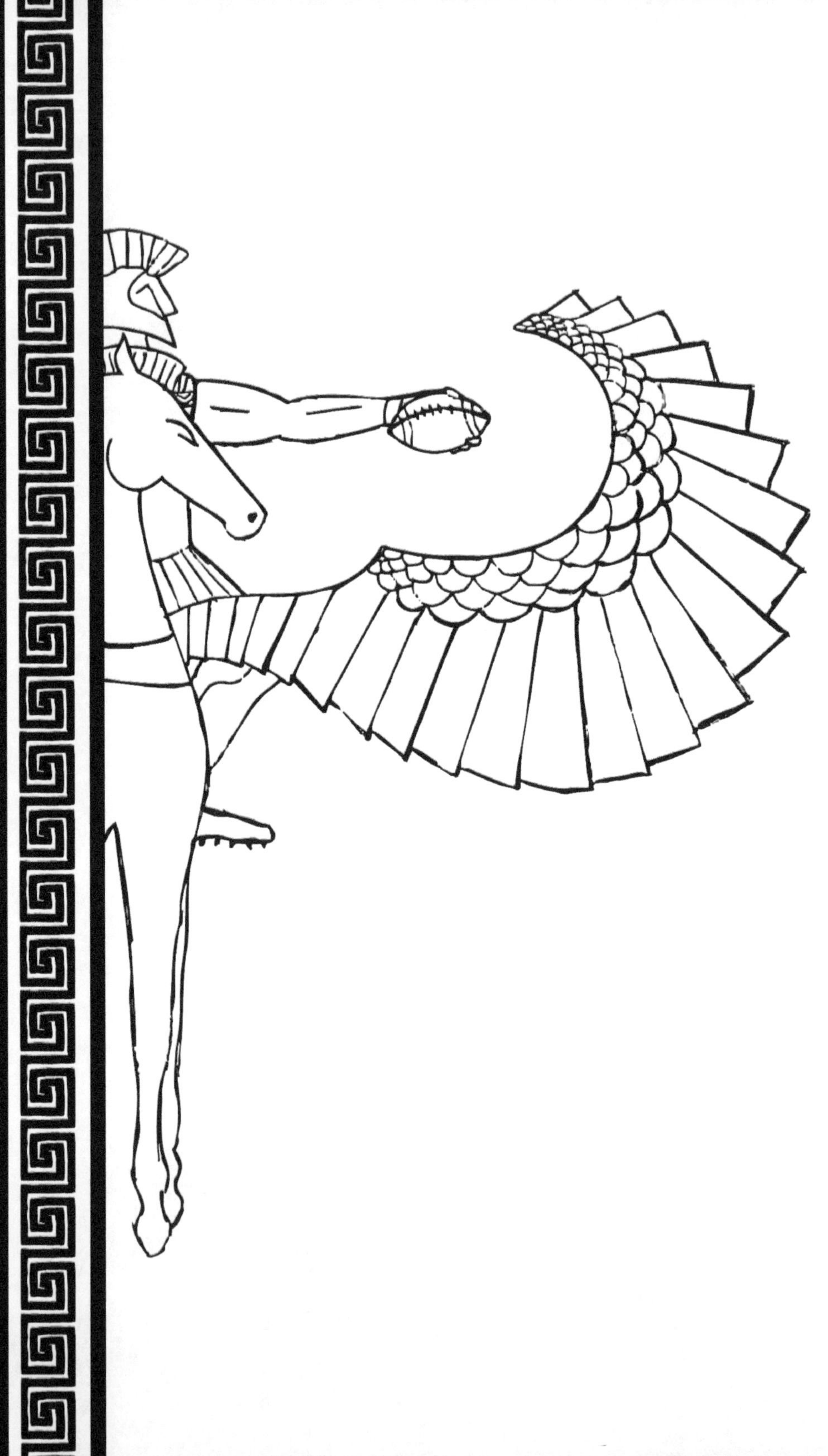

THE NINTH GAME

THE DESTRUCTION OF THE "TROJANS" FROM CAPTAIN JACK HIGH SCHOOL BY "THE FOUR HORSEMEN," IN THE NINTH FOOTBALL GAME OF THE SEASON, BY THE SCORE OF "TWENTY-EIGHT TO NOTHING," MAY NOT HAVE BEEN UNLIKE THE MYTHICAL DESTRUCTION OF THE ANCIENT "CITY OF TROY," CHRONICLED BY HOMER IN HIS EPIC POEM, ENTITLED "THE ILIAD," BECAUSE, AMONG A NUMBER OF OTHER, SEEMINGLY, MYTHICAL THINGS, IT WAS THE RESULT OF DECEIT IN EACH INSTANCE, ANCIENT AND CONTEMPORARY, BY "HORSE-RELATED" THINGS.

Well, without a clear answer to some of those kinds of transcendental questions, at least at this point in our story, possibly we need to leave the "blinding snowstorm" and the "winged feet" behind, with the defeated caricature of a "discolored, snowbound eagle." Because the undefeated and untied "Boys From Across

The River," at least at that point in the season, were about to be confronted at the end of the following week, on another Friday evening, by the "Blue and Gold" of Captain Jack High School, known, at the time, as the "Trojans." And in case you are wondering, those "Trojans" were not hailing from the ancient "City of Troy," but, rather, from the far more contemporaneous town of Mount Union, Pennsylvania.

Although the name of the opposing team changed on the following Friday evening, along with their colors, not much else did, not over the entire four quarters of that ninth football game. Once again, "The Seven Blocks of Granite," not years ago at Fordham University, but over the previous Friday evenings, dominated the line of scrimmage, and for all four quarters, too. That, likely, accounted for the inability of the "Trojans" to do much of anything geographically, let alone arithmetically, by the end of that one-sided affair. They simply had no offensive answer for that "granite-like line," confronting them throughout the entire game. It was not unlike being besieged in their very own stadium, not unlike the mythical fate suffered by their classical counterparts in the "City of Troy," as chronicled in the epic Greek Poem, "The Iliad," by Homer, and, subsequently, the epic Latin Poem, "The Aeneid," by Virgil.

Meanwhile, in the absence of any real offense, over the entire four quarters of that game, at least to speak about, by the contemporaneous "Trojans," on the "field of play," as they say in the game, "The Four Horsemen," Schiavo, Goodman, Englert and Johnson, "rode again," as it has been historically said, except that, in this instance, they were clad in the "purple and white uniforms" of the "Bobcats" from Lock Haven High School, playing decades, or was it really millennia, later, in the J. Arlington Painter Stadium. Without a description of what that meant on the "field of play," as they say in the game, seemingly unnecessary at this point in the story, let me simply point out that the "Trojan" goal line was under "siege," any number of times, by "The Four Horsemen," who actually crossed it on four separate occasions, by four different methods, over the course of that entire game.

The result of such a marauding backfield and such an immovable line was the continuation of an undefeated and untied season, by the score of "twenty eight," for the besieging "Bobcats," and "nothing" for the besieged "Trojans." Having said that, the score, if not the game, itself, resulted in a change, somewhat, in a growing myth, by becoming somewhat classical in nature, largely because of a claim by the contemporary "Trojans," at the end of that one-sided affair, that the defense, displayed throughout the entire four quarters of the game by "The Seven Blocks of Granite," was "Herculean" in nature. And in their contemporaneous opinion, that mythical aberration, reoccurring now,

millennia later, certainly explained why their "blue and white team" was unable to score, not once, not over the course of the entire football game, let alone "move the ball," as it has been said, but not necessarily in classical circumstances, beyond their own forty one yard line, by any means, whatsoever.

Similarly, the contemporaneous "Trojans" also complained that the unbelievable offensive display by "The Four Horsemen," over all four quarters of that football game, was predicated, in large part, upon deception, not unlike the mythical one perpetrated upon their classical counterparts in the siege of the ancient City of Troy. Not unlike that classical deception, perpetrated by something resembling a gigantic horse, those in this instance, according to that contemporary complaint, were perpetrated by "The Four Horsemen," millennia later, including Bill Goodman, still playing at left halfback; Bob Crissman, playing, sometimes, at right halfback; and Dave Johnson, still playing at quarterback. In the retrospective opinion of the contemporaneous "Trojans," those three football players succeeded, by various forms of deception, in scoring touchdowns by runs of varying, but not insignificant, distances!

In fact, forgetting, for the moment, about the classical deception involving the City of Troy, one could easily say, with respect to the current season, that Dave Johnson's deceptive brilliance, in calling plays at the quarterback position, served in no small part for his team being undefeated and untied at that point in the season. Moreover, it also likely explains, if nothing else does, his later-in-life success as a dental surgeon, if you do not mind a little bit of noteworthy repetition!

Incidentally, but no less materially, John Englert kicked four field goals in that game, never missing one of them, which may also be explained by a myth, although not necessarily classical in nature, especially when considering his contemporaneous consistency, over all nine games played at that point in the season, and, especially as a high school athlete on a scholastic gridiron at the time. Well, whatever it may possibly be, or have been, it certainly was not inconsistent with an ever-growing myth, at least from an historical perspective, about the legendary play of "The Boys From Across The River," who seemed to appear, weekly, that season, "in purple and white," to confront another football team on another high school gridiron, in one town or another, on another Friday evening, somewhere in central Pennsylvania.

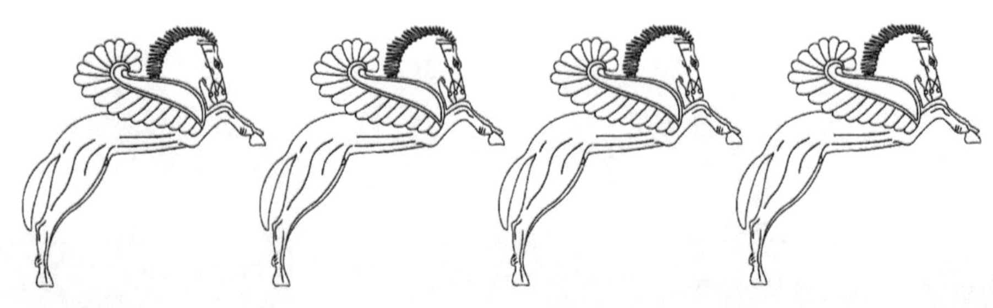

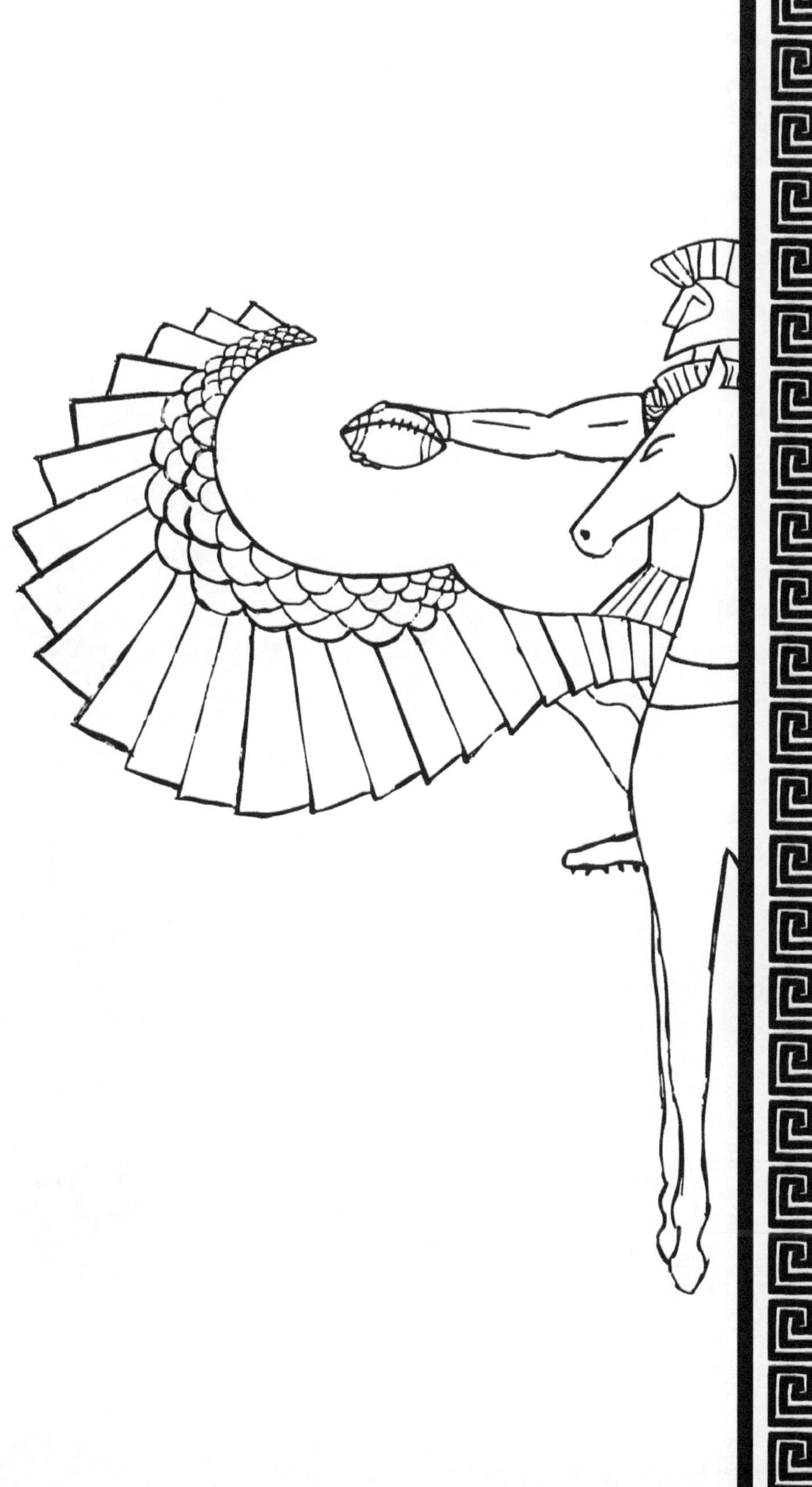

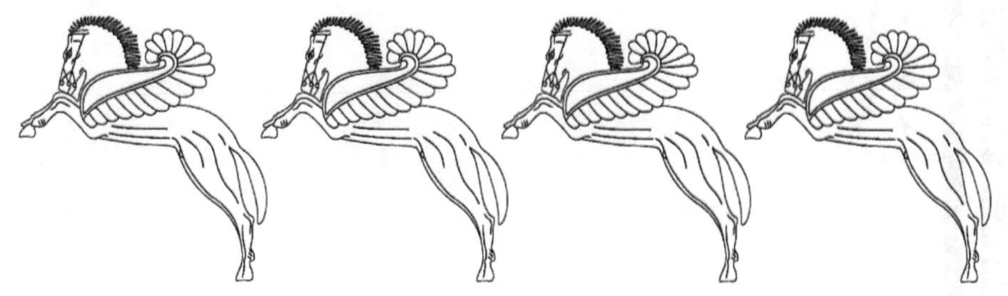

THE FINAL GAME

THE SURPRISING VICTORY BY THE HIGH SCHOOL IN THE TOWN OF LOCK HAVEN OVER THE PERENNIALLY UNDEFEATED HIGH SCHOOL IN WILLIAMSPORT, A CITY ROUGHLY SEVEN TIMES LARGER, BY A "TWENTY TO SIX" SCORE, IN THE FINAL GAME OF THAT SEASON, BECAME MORE THAN LEGENDARY IN SUBSEQUENT FOLKLORE, BECAUSE OF THE NATURE OF THAT LARGER HIGH SCHOOL, THE NATURE OF THAT LARGER FOOTBALL TEAM, THE NATURE OF THAT FOOTBALL GAME, ITSELF, WHICH WAS AS UNREAL AS THOSE PRECEDING IT, THE NATURE OF A FOOTBALL TEAM KNOWN AS "THE BOYS FROM ACROSS THE RIVER," AND, FINALLY, THE NATURE OF A NUMBER OF OTHER UNREAL, IF NOT SURREAL, THINGS, ASSOCIATED THEREWITH, NOT EXCLUDING, AN "AGELESS CHANT," A "PECULIAR MARCHING BAND," A "TIMELESS FIGHT SONG," AND, EVEN, THE "SEVEN, ALWAYS SEVEN, CHEERLEADERS," IF NOT A NO-LONGER-EXISTING "OVERHEAD BRIDGE."

Still, myths, like their legendary counterparts, have a way of, historically, retreating in the face of reality, especially over time, and reality was about to confront a growing-legend, at the end of the following week, in the form of a football team in "Cherry and White," called the "Millionaires," from a much larger and more heralded High School in the City of Williamsport.

In fact, the High School in Williamsport, a city of nearly fifty thousand at the time, was proportionally larger than the one in Lock Haven, a town not much larger than seventy-five hundred at the time, which, of course, was nearly seven times smaller than its, nearby, urban counterpart. Compounding that proportional difference, or that demographic distinction, in their respective communities, if not in their respective High Schools, confronting the legend-makers at the time, the "Millionaires" had not lost a game in nearly three years, and, consistent therewith, they were undefeated at that point in this season, too. In that regard, they had already ruined the season of such traditional football powers as the "Mountain Lions" from Altoona High School, the "Pioneers" from John Harris High School and the "Tigers" from William Penn High School, the latter two High Schools being located in the City of Harrisburg, which, of course, was the Capitol of the State of Pennsylvania.

I am not even going to list the other high schools of a comparable size and athletic reputation throughout the State, whose well known football teams had also suffered a loss that year to the "Cherry and White." In short, that magnificent football team from "Bill-Town," whose football currency was calculated in the "millions," at least nominally, if not metaphorically, had been terrifying their opposition on high school gridirons for years. That successful football history, if not the pride generated thereby, not to mention the athletic prowess upon which it was based, without even considering the number of players at each position on that team, were, likely, the reasons for their perennial success!

Not surprisingly, the "Bobcats" had not put a dent in that incredible history since 1924, fully thirty years ago, which, incidentally, was the last time that the "Purple and White" had finished a season without any form of a blemish on their football record. Nonetheless, "The Boys From Across The River," apparently, decided to forget about all of those unsuccessful years, involving all of their defeated predecessors, and complete their season unbeaten and untied, if not continue a justifiable legend associated therewith. To do so, of course, they had to defeat the "Cherry and White," with all of that "history," and all of that "pride," and all of that "athletic prowess," not to mention all of those numbers," at every position, too, and in their very own stadium as well, which was monstrous, with all of those local people, continually, cheering for the hometown team, or, if you will, the "Millionaires."

Nevertheless, unintimidated, or only slightly so, they elected to kickoff to, at least, three of them, the "history," the "pride," and the "athletic prowess" but, fortunately, not to all of those "numbers," just to those on the first team. The other two teams, of course, were remaining on the "bench," awaiting their opportunity to enter the game, at a later point, possibly in the second half, in order to "wear down" an adversary, like the one facing them, with just one team and a few reserves from the junior varsity. And, thereafter, a football game began, with surprising aspects, based on legendary considerations, which became a part of folklore, shortly thereafter, and, possibly, mythology, seventy years later.

Having said that, I should also acknowledge that the legendary season of the visiting aspirants, characterized by an indescribable performance on a high school gridiron, any high school gridiron, at least up to that point in time, became anything but legendary for nearly the entire first half on that one. In fact, that legendary play, associated with all nine of the previous games that season, nearly came to an end, at least offensively, during the first two quarters of that game.

Without undertaking a repetitive description of what that meant on the "field of play," as they say in the game, during that challenging period of time, suffice it to say, that whatever it was that had once enthralled almost everyone from their hometown with an uncanny ability to score, on almost anyone, by almost any means, in almost any situation, at almost any time, in a football game, nearly came to an end before that half had concluded. That daunting fact caused everyone seated in that foreign stadium, wearing something in a "purple and white," to remember, if, by chance, they had forgotten, over that uncomfortable period of time, why the other team was called the "Millionaires."

On the other hand, history, in the form of "Cherry and White," began to, offensively, "repeat itself," as the Spanish Philosopher, George Santayana, had predicted. Now outfitted in those vibrant colors, it began to, resolutely, "march down the field," as they often say in those kinds of football games, likely to no one's surprise, not even to the two combatants on the field, at least not at that point, anyway; moreover, they nearly scored!

Somewhere near the thirteen or fourteen yard line of a rapidly diminishing legend, however, an errant handoff ended up in the eager hands of a charging lineman, wearing a "purple and white jersey" and a disbelieving expression on his face, which, incidentally, matched the faces of nearly everyone else in a football uniform, irrespective of color, on the "field of play" at the time. And with that unpredictable fact, especially if you happened to be a student of history, the first attempt by the "Millionaires" to confirm Santayana's renown precept, and to "repeat itself," or "themselves," as the case may be, on that football field and on that day and in that game, came to a precipitous, if not an inglorious, end; interestingly enough, however, a wavering legend, at least at that point in the game, did not!

Nevertheless, that "wavering legend" was unable to even gain a first down thereafter, following three futile attempts to do so. Consequently, the ball was, subsequently, kicked, once again, to the "Millionaires," who were, eagerly, awaiting another opportunity to inflict mayhem on their, supposedly, legendary visitors. And, I should add, confirm a history that was about to unfold, or continue, as the case may be, in which those visitors would become nothing more than pathetic-participants.

Well, to a certain extent, that almost became an historical fact, because the "Cherry and White," methodically, marched down the field, all over again, in a "series of downs," as they historically say in the game, in order to ensure the continuation of an historical outcome. This time, however, the "Millionaires," still outfitted in the same distinctive colors and with the same historical intent, "bogged-down," as they say, around the twenty four or twenty five yard line. And following three more attempts at making history, or ensuring the continuance thereof, with only inconsequential results, given an opposing line that was becoming formidable, although not yet legendary, the "Millionaires" did the unthinkable, at least historically so: they flinched and kicked a field goal at that point, which, of course, was on their fourth down!

Notwithstanding that flinching fact, there was still a lot of pride wrapped up in those "cherry and white uniforms," which probably explains the subsequent inability of their "purple and white visitors" to do much more than gain a few inconsequential first downs, following the receipt of a well kicked football. Realizing their plight, if not their challenging field position, thereafter, they decided to kick the ball, once again, to an awaiting history, intent on "repeating itself," and with an actual touchdown this time!

Unfortunately, however, their historical movement down the field, admittedly with a seeming inevitability, all over again, came at a much slower pace and at a much higher price this time, largely because of the resurgence, if not the resurrection of "The Seven Blocks of Granite," as well as an associated legend with respect thereto. Becoming more than aware of both, at or near the twenty two yard line, because of an inability to "move the ball" much further, as they often say in such situations, no matter what they tried, over three frustrating downs, history, in the "form of cherry and white," began to no longer believe in itself, at least not to the same extent. And, consequently, it did the unthinkable once again, by kicking another field goal at that point, from over thirty yards away this time.

Consequently, the score at that point, which happened to be the end of the first quarter, was "six to nothing," in favor of the mighty "Millionaires," which, when you think about it, was, technically, not inconsistent with history, the "cherry and white kind," and for years, too! But when you think about it even more, that may not be historically accurate, because kicking field goals was not the way that the magnificent "Millionaires" had been striking fear into opposing football programs on high school gridirons . . . and for years, too. Moreover, those teams were, generally, part of football programs that were much

larger and, seemingly, more formidable than the one confronting them now. And that consequential fact, or those consequential facts, even at the end of the first quarter, in which a growing legend, in the form of an undefeated and untied football team, was only losing by such an inconsequential score to a virtually unchallenged history, for years, possessed by the miraculous "Millionaires," was, to most of those on the field, if not off of it, too, inconceivable, if not unbelievable!

The impact of that "unbelievable," if not "inconceivable," fact, as well as the equilibrium, seemingly, created thereby, between those two respective football teams, newly discovered at that point in the athletic competition, likely by both squads, probably explains the inability of ether one of them to do very much of anything, thereafter, in the second quarter of that game, not of any consequence, anyway. And that is notwithstanding some very serious efforts to the contrary by both of them, at least not until that period had nearly expired.

At that significant point, the "Moose" nearly destroyed a left halfback, wearing a "grass-stained cherry and white jersey," on or about their forty-nine yard line, while trying to run through the middle of a very stalwart line, having now regained most of its "granite-like" characteristics, causing the ball, which he had been previously carrying, to, literally, pop up into the air. And to make matters historically worse for the "cherry and white squad" and legendarily better for the "purple and white one," and at the very same time, too, a very alert moose-like creature immediately snatched it, before letting it hit the ground. Then, wheeling around, at about the same time, he began to lumber down the football field, while carrying his "prized-possession," as it has often been said, although not ordinarily in that context, not to mention a few of the, now, panicking, "cherry and white team," as well as a very significant part of their undefeated history, too, all the way down to their sixteen yard line!

Following that unpredictable event, a rejuvenated backfield, trying to reestablish themselves as "The Four Horsemen," clawed their way, metaphorically speaking, over the remaining sixteen yards, in a "series of downs," as they often say in reference to those kinds of situations and in those kinds of football games, to an historically untrammeled end zone, with Bill Goodman, still playing at left halfback, carrying the "pigskin," not to mention the disbelief of the hometown crowd, over the last, several, agonizing-yards. And to add despair to their disbelief, John Englert ensured, by an extra point kick, that the hometown team would leave the "field of battle," so to speak, slightly behind at the end of that half, the first half of that unpredictable football game, by a score of "seven to six," probably for the first time in history, or, at least, that part of it that anyone could actually remember, anyway!

The significance of that, seemingly, insignificant numerical difference, however, was measured by far more than merely an arithmetic number; it was measured by a self-confidence factor, which was increasing by that number on the one hand and decreasing by it on the other. The reality of that fact, or of that factor, or of that

number, or of that significant difference, became far more manifest as the second half began.

It actually began with a kickoff to a group of reinvigorated "purple and white players," intent on revising history, or, at least, continuing a legend, and for the remainder of the game, too. And, unfortunately, for that history, but, fortunately, for that legend, the ball was fielded by none other than John Edward Englert, who was, generally, far less inclined to engage in introspection, prevailing nearly everywhere else on that field at the time, and far more inclined to engage in action, often unreasonably so, sort of like the proverbial, "bull in the china shop kind," as it is often said about that kind of behavior!

Consistent therewith, John even outran his blockers, along with a great majority of the other team as well, although to be uncomfortably accurate about the situation, he did run over a few of them, too, who, unfortunately, got in his way, to the astonishment of nearly everyone else on the field, stopping only when there was no more field in which to run. And for good measure, he added to the indignity, if not the score, by kicking an extra point, following, of course, the hearty congratulations of his astonished teammates, obviously for that, "bull in the china shop" reason, or if you prefer a more sportsmen-like phraseology, that remarkable return!

Something happened, following that ruinous return, likely to both teams, which is sort of difficult to put into words; if nothing else, however, it could possibly be explained by the score, which had now become "fourteen to six," in favor of the "Purple and White," and which was more "legendary" than "historical." And for that legendary reason, if not for that "bullish-return," both teams began to believe that one of them was likely better than the other, at least on that field and on that day, if not on any field and on any day. And I am not speaking here about any form of "currencies," either, not at that turning point in the game!

Nevertheless, following that disastrous kickoff return, and the consequences thereof to their team, not to mention to their season, and, maybe, even to their history, if not to their historical effort in this instance, the "Millionaires" quickly recovered, by recalling why they were not called the "Thousands" or even the "Hundreds." It was, of course, because of what they had historically been, as a result of whom they had historically beaten, on almost any gridiron, at almost anytime, and for years; moreover, regaining some of their justifiable pride, thereby, they began to act accordingly.

Likely, for that reason, or those reasons, the rest of that quarter, the third quarter of that football game, and nearly all of the remaining one, were comparatively uneventful, because neither one of those two teams seemed to be able to change their current situation, either on the field or on the scoreboard, or, for that matter, in the more surreal world of psychology, even though the score remained, at that point, in favor of the legend-makers. Nevertheless, even with the possibility of an undefeated and untied season hovering over them, if not on the field, itself, at the expense of an historical blip to the record of those on the "other side of the ball," so to speak, the legend-makers were unable to do anything more, over that period of time, to contribute to the unrealistic aspect of what they seemed to have been accomplishing!

That, of course, was largely because the football players from that gargantuan high school to the northeast, wearing a fairly distinctive, "cherry and white uniform," did not know how to lose, which may have been one of the reasons why they rarely ever did, which may be somewhat repetitive and circuitous, but it is also quite accurate! And even though those on a football team from a more diminutive high school to the southwest, now wearing a fairly indistinctive, "purple and white uniform," tried to ignore that historical fact, or, for that matter, all of those historical facts, it was becoming ever more difficult to accomplish, especially at that stage of the game. That was largely because, if nothing else, those who were now confronting them in the second half, at each position on the field, seemed to be changing, with each quarter, by substitution, if not by magic!

Likely for those numerical reasons, or, at least, the substitution thereof, throughout the remainder of that half, which, in reality, was the second half of that football game, the losing side, at least at that point in the game, was not willing to, metaphorically, "give an inch," as they like to say, although not necessarily in football games, not geographically, not arithmetically, and not even psychologically.

Actually, not until the waning minutes of the game, when, inexplicably, Bob Crissman, substituting for an exhausted, "Chub" Schiavo, at the right halfback position, disappeared, quite literally, into the interior of the opposing line, now in a raggedy and indistinct "cherry and white," following a routine handoff from his quarterback, Dave Johnson. And following a few indescribable minutes, in which he seemed to have been engulfed by nearly everything in a "cherry and white uniform," he reappeared, almost magically, if not miraculously, and, possibly, even mythically, with the ball tucked, neatly, under both arms, on the other side of the line of scrimmage, the historic side, that is. And, thereafter, with comparatively "fresh legs," as they like to say near the end of football games, like that one, he outran a bewildered and exhausted secondary, seemingly stationary at that point in the contest, which had once been historic, but not anymore, for a sixty seven yard sprint, unbelievably so, into a, formerly, rarified end zone!

John Englert's failure to convert on the extra point try, following that miraculous run, was almost as unusual as the run, itself, which, of course, you must have realized, at least by this point in the story. In fact, his otherwise consistency, if not his continued ability, at kicking extra points, was so unusual on those scholastic football fields at the time, where extra points were normally achieved by running or, less frequently, by passing, as you must know by now, that, by midseason, he was periodically characterized as "The Toe," by the Sports Editor for the *Lock Haven Express*.

Shortly after that missed extra point, both teams left the field, one with the first loss that it had suffered in years, which became an historic fact; the other with an undefeated and untied season, by, among a number of other incredulous things, winning that football game against the mighty "Millionaires," by a "twenty to six" score, which became a legendary fact. And given what had already transpired over the course of that season, in the nine previous games, that legendary victory over the "Cherry and White," subsequently became the subject of folklore in those mountainous regions, and following a great amount of discussion and disbelief, relating to all ten of those legendary games, the subject of mythology, years later.

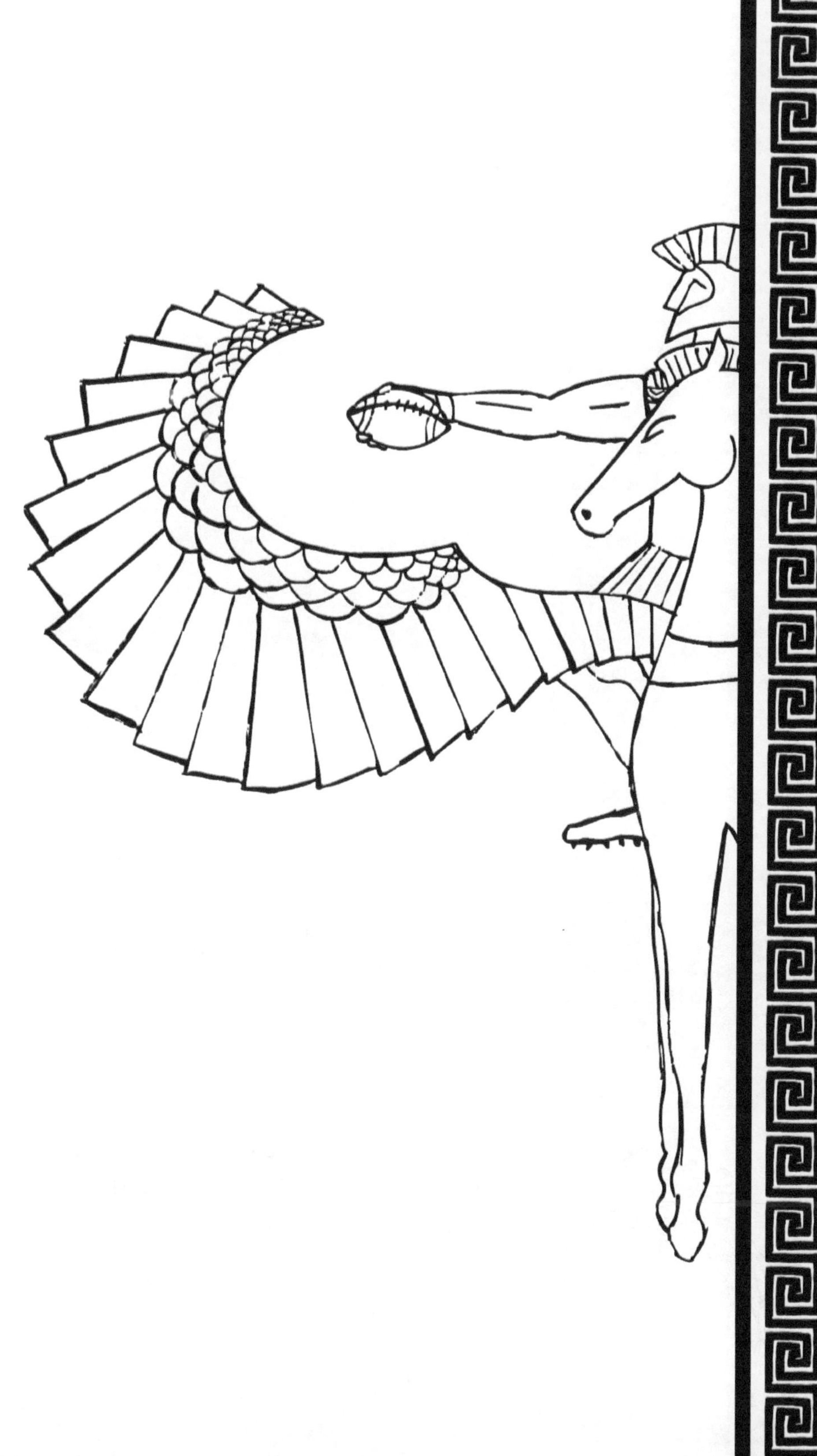

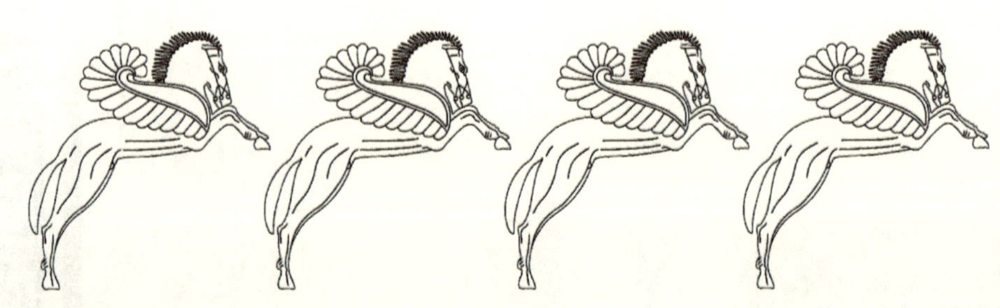

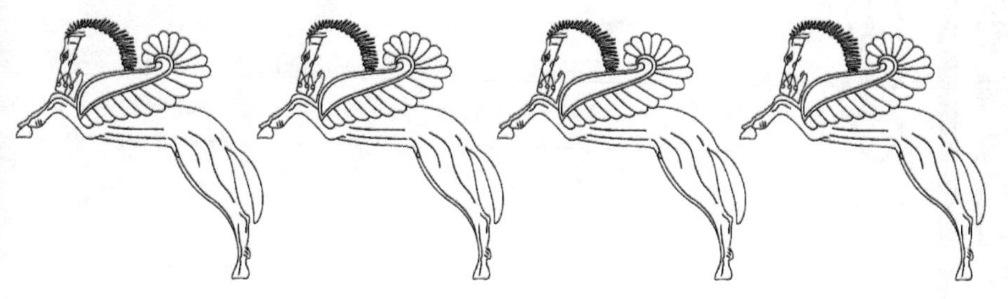

THE CONCLUSION

THOSE UNREALISTIC conclusions, not easily reached, are not simply because the team ended that season unbeaten and untied; they are also because of whom they had beaten and how they did it, which was, in many of those instances, unbelievable at the time and, likely, for all time!

For one, they had just left the "field of play," in which they had beaten the vaunted "Millionaires" of Williamsport High School, in their very own, very impressive, "cherry and white stadium," too. Something that had not been done in years, not even by some of the larger and, seemingly, more impressive football programs in the State, representing high schools that were, roughly, six or even seven times larger than their own. And that certainly included high schools like the "Mountain Lions" of Altoona High School and the "Pioneers" of John Harris High School.

What's more, only two teams, the "Maroon and Steel" of Lewistown High School and the "Red Raiders" of Bellefonte High School, both of whom were unbeaten at the time, managed to score more than one touchdown against that monumental defense. And the second one occurred, in each one of those two games, against the junior varsity, playing the remainder of the game after it was, essentially, "put out of reach," as they say, by the varsity. And if that were not impressive enough, the opposing team could not even score at all in six of the other ten games that season. Even the mighty "Millionaires" of Williamsport High School, huge and impressive by local standards, could only muster two field goals, or six points, over the entire four quarters of that game.

Although those facts may appear to be incredible, especially over an entire season, they are explained, in part, by the nature of the football players on that defensive line. Every one of them were athletically gifted; although some were more so in "defending against the run," as they like to say, and, on the other hand, some were more so in "rushing the passer," as they also like to say in the game. But three of them, located in the interior of that impressive line, were so talented at their respective positions that it really did not make much difference whether they were "defending against the run," or "rushing the passer," or even a combination thereof.

Two of those players, Bill Karch and Tom Toner, playing at the left and right guard positions, respectively, on the interior of that defensive line, were so talented at their respective positions, in defending against both the "run" and the "pass," that they were selected by a statewide committee of journalists to be a member of the interior line that season on the "All State Football Team." Moreover, of even more consequence, both of them were selected, even though they were members of the same interior line, although at opposite ends thereon, on the same high school football team that season, which was a phenomena that was almost unheard of prior to that time.

Possibly of even more significance to this incredible high school football story, or the unrealistic aspect of that high school football team, there was, actually, a third individual on the interior of that defensive line, Jack "Moose" Houser, playing between the other two interior linemen, at the center position, who may well have been the very best player on that defensive line, if not on the team, itself, according to a number of local journalists. In reaching that, admittedly, extravagant conclusion . . . given the nature of the other two players on the interior of that defensive line . . . one of those journalists even went so far as to conclude that Jack Houser, given his size, speed and overall athletic ability, may well have been one of the very best high school football players that season at the center position in the State of Pennsylvania, if not in the Nation, itself.

Well, whatever may be the case, I would be remiss if I did not also point out that a fourth player on that unparalleled defensive line, Jan Bennett, was not only an excellent defensive player, but he may also have been, in the estimation of a number of those journalists, one of the best pass-catching left ends on a scholastic gridiron in the country that year. And as the outstanding member of an unbeaten and untied basketball team that year, he may also have been, at six feet seven inches in height, one of the greatest basketball players that year in the State of Pennsylvania, according to the same journalists, especially considering his subsequent selection, by a statewide committee, as an "All State" basketball player, following that season.

Largely, because of those four outstanding reasons, unparalleled at the time on a high school gridiron, any high school gridiron, anywhere, not to mention the remaining members of that outstanding defensive line, it was, in the end, nearly impossible to score on the "Seven Blocks of Granite," over the course of that entire season.

On the other hand, "The Four Horsemen" were able to score on anyone, at anytime, by, virtually, any means whatsoever, even against the perennially great "Maroon and Steel" of Lewistown High School and the perennially undefeated "Millionaires" of Williamsport High School. And that kind of offensive success, against those kinds of football teams, if not all kinds of football teams, large and small, can be explained by the talent, if not the diverse forms thereof, in that highly unusual backfield, rarely ever found on a high school gridiron, certainly not at the time!

For one, the speed and open field running ability of "Chub" Schiavo, playing at the right halfback position, was unmatched on a high school gridiron, in the opinion of a local newspaper editor, not only in his own backfield, but elsewhere, too, in central Pennsylvania, if not in the State of Pennsylvania. And that editor went on to note, almost as an afterthought, that the "innate athletic ability" of that young man "exceeded the norm," not only at that position on the football field, but as a forward on the "hardwood" of an undefeated basketball team, later that year, as well as an infielder on a baseball diamond, years earlier, playing for the "All Stars" from Lock Haven, Pennsylvania, who, as you will recall, were able to beat Pensacola, Florida, "six to five," to win the "Little League World Series."

On the other hand, Bill Goodman, playing at the left halfback position, was a much larger and more powerful running back in that multitalented backfield. His size, in fact, exceeded every other member of that backfield, if not every one of the linemen, too, with the possible exception of the "Moose," whose anatomical dimensions were nearly unique, as I have already intimated, on a high school gridiron at the time. And that overwhelming size probably explains why he was consistently able to run through the line of scrimmage, rather than around it, no matter what may have been the name of the opposing team, or, more specifically, the nature of their defensive linemen.

Interestingly enough, however, John Englert, playing at the fullback position, was nearly as powerful, as a running back, although not quite as large as Bill Goodman; but he was still larger and, seemingly, stronger than most fullbacks on a high school gridiron that season in the State of Pennsylvania, according to a comment made by that statewide committee. But what made him so formidable, as a running back, was not simply his size and strength, which, of course, had already been noted by that committee, it was, in their opinion, his, peculiarly, "enraged running style," not unlike that of a proverbial, "bull moose," especially in the open field, where he often ran over members of an opposing secondary, rather than trying to simply avoid them. But his real value to that multidimensional backfield, if not to that legendary team, itself, lie in his multiple offensive talents, according to the same committee, which were continually on display throughout each game that season.

In that regard, it was noted that, notwithstanding a highly competent quarterback, he may well have been the most accurate passer on the team, especially in delivering long passes, which he did quite often, in nearly every game that season. And that was, ordinarily, quite surprising to opposing teams, in the opinion of the same committee members, which were not used to playing against a fullback, who was passing the ball nearly as often as he was running it. And, of course, his consistency at kicking extra points in every game that season became legendary, throughout the journalistic world in central Pennsylvania, because most football teams at a high school level, at the time, accomplished that after-the-score possibility by a running or, less frequently, by a passing effort, likely because of a lack of that kind of a kicking capability.

It is also true that Dave Johnson, in his play at the quarterback position, likely possessed as much athletic ability as the other members of that multitalented backfield . . . with the possible exception of "Chub" Schiavo, who, of course, was recognized, nearly everywhere in that area, as "one of a kind" . . . which probably explains why he, subsequently, became the best scholastic wrestler that year at one hundred and fifty-four pounds in the State of Pennsylvania, never having been "taken down" or even "reversed," over his high school career, as they often say in the wrestling world.

Having said that, however, I would be remiss if I did not point out that Dave's mental acuity may well have even exceeded his athletic prowess, metaphorically speaking, that is, which may explain, somewhat, why he was placed at the quarterback position, directing that multidimensional offense, by his Coach. It also may explain his success, in doing so, over the entire season of a football team, which was so full of outstanding players, with talents so diverse in the backfield, that it was nearly impossible for an opposing team to "key," as they often say in the game, on any one of them, over the course of a game or even over the course of a season. Indeed, that innate mental acuity, so manifest on a football field, especially during that unbeaten and untied season, may also serve as an explanation, as I have previously pointed out, for his later in life success as a dental surgeon!

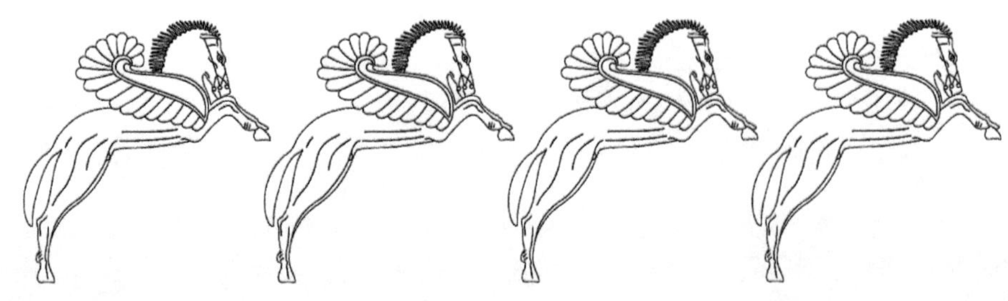

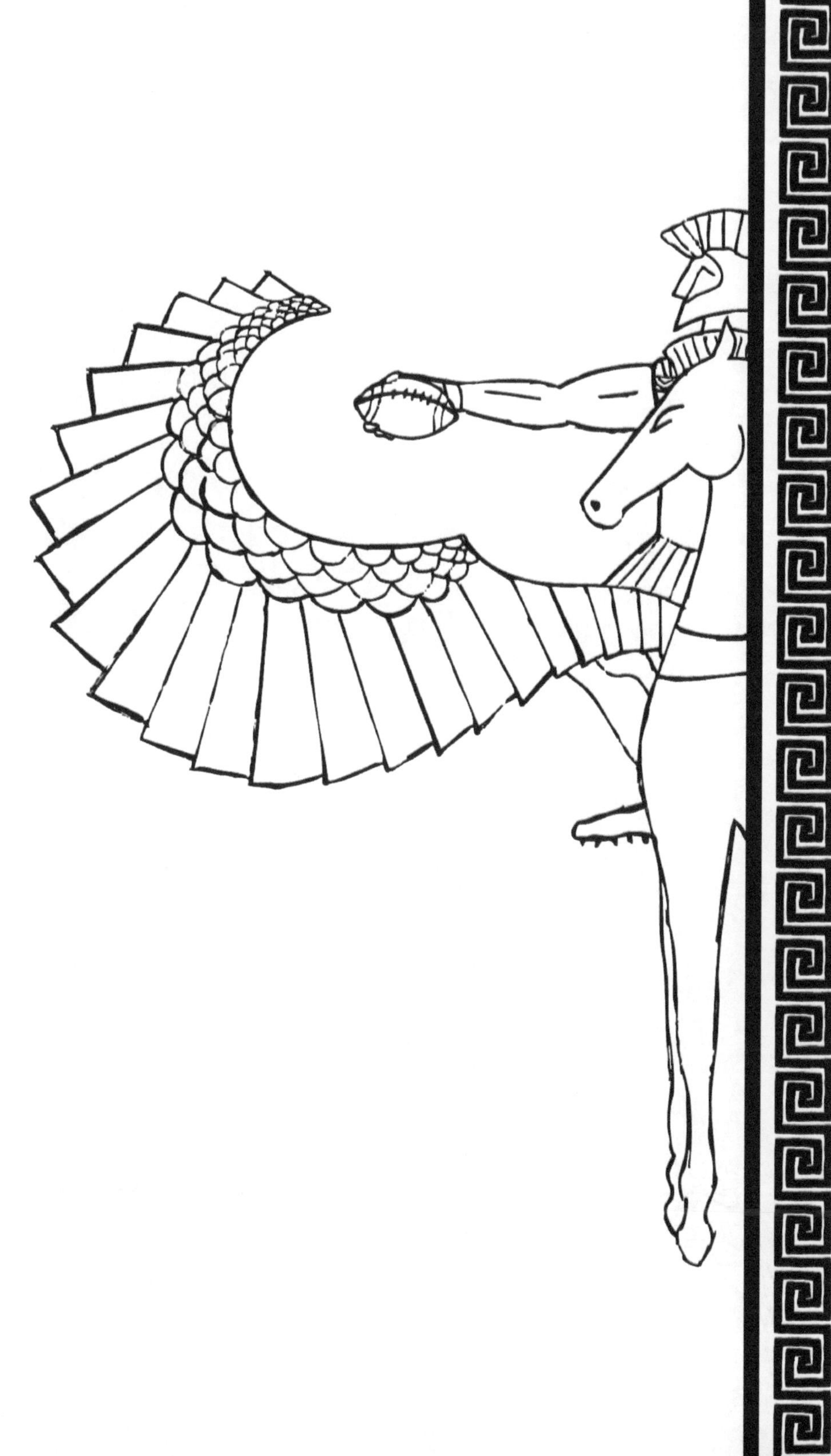

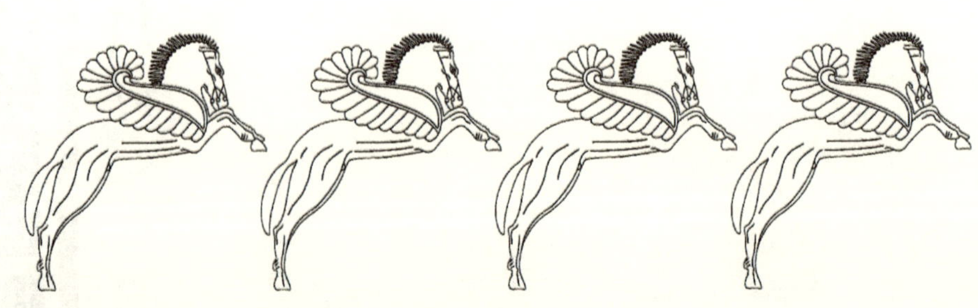

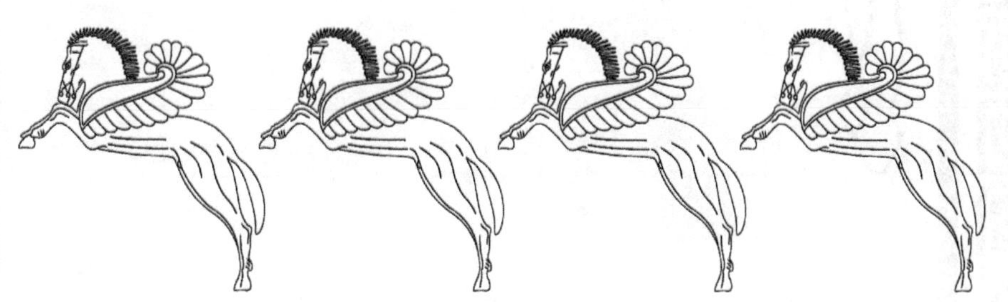

THE AFTERWORD

Following the end of that football season, the unbeaten and untied "Bobcats," wearing the "Purple and White" of Lock Haven High School, were declared the "Champions of the Susquehanna League," the "Outstanding Team of the Central Counties League" and in "Second Place in The Western Conference," consisting, essentially, of much larger high schools in the Western part of the State.

Individual recognition went to Bill Karch, who was selected on the "First Team of the Associated Press All Pennsylvania Scholastic Football Team," at "Left Guard;" Tom Toner, who was selected on the "Second Team of the Associated Press All Pennsylvania Scholastic Football Team," at "Right Guard" and Dave Johnson, who was an "Honorable Mention Selection," at "Quarterback," on the "Associated Press All Pennsylvania Scholastic Football Team."

Just as significant, if not more so, Bill Karch and Jack ("Moose") Houser were subsequently awarded full athletic scholarships to play football in the fall of that year for the "Seminoles" of Florida State University. Interestingly, in that respect, "The Boys" often said that the "Moose" was one of the outstanding players on a football team that was, quite obviously, full of outstanding players. Apparently, the Athletic Director of Florida State University agreed. Not to be ignored, Dave Johnson, subsequently, received a full athletic scholarship to wrestle in the fall of that year for the University of Pittsburgh; Jan Bennett, on the other hand, received a full athletic scholarship to play basketball in the fall of that year for an equally renown university somewhere in the South; John Englert, interestingly enough, played football in the fall of that year for a smaller college, tuition free, in central Pennsylvania; and Charles "Chub" Schiaivo . . . who was a forward on the undefeated basketball team later that year, as well as an outstanding member of the Lock Haven, Pennsylvania "All Star Team," prior thereto, which won the "Little League World Series," by beating Pensacola, Florida, six to five . . . was posthumously selected to be a member of the Clinton County Athletic Hall of Fame.

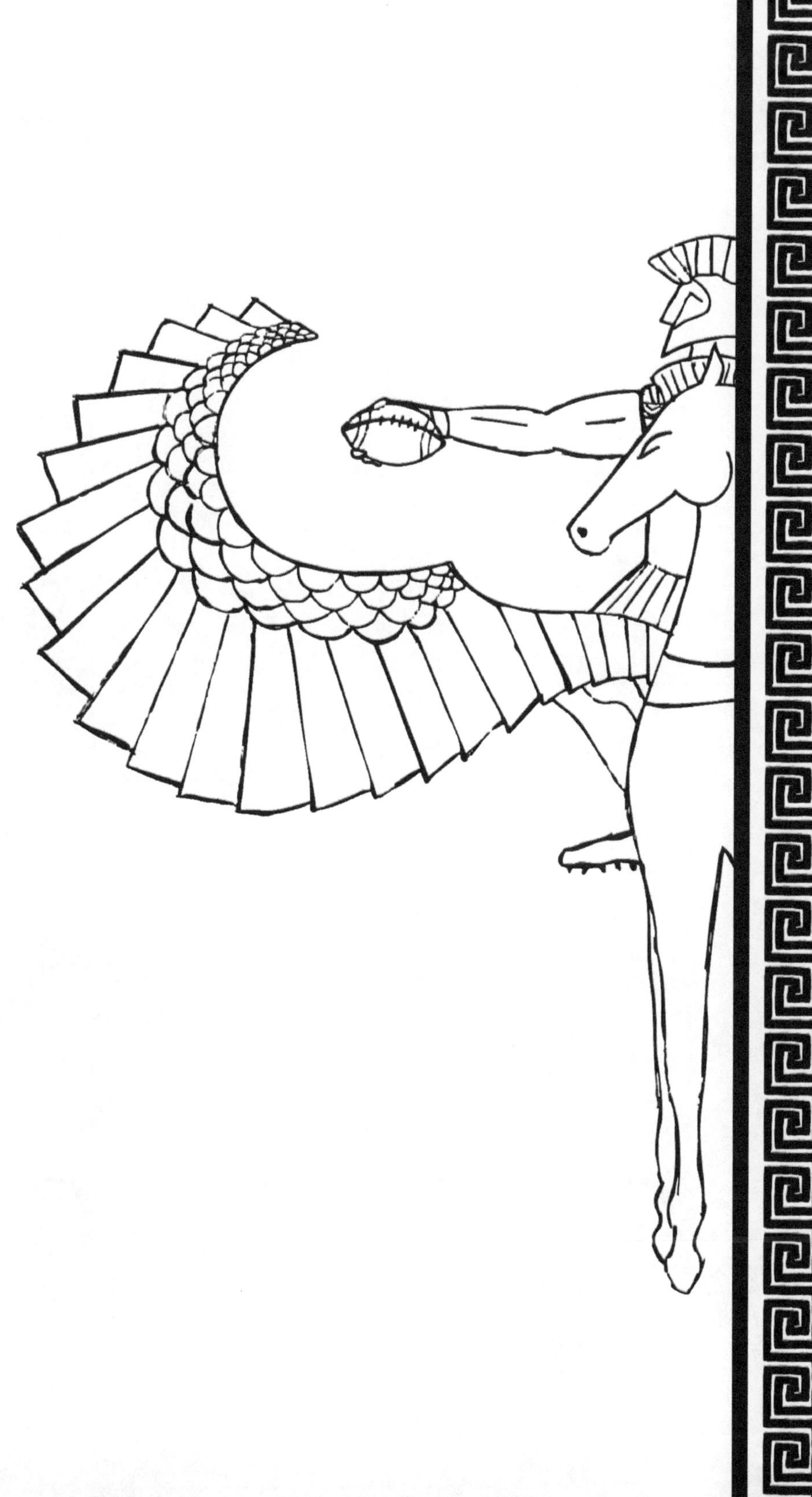

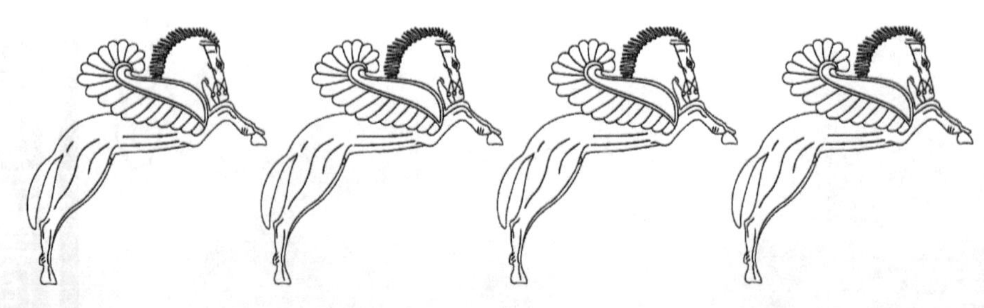

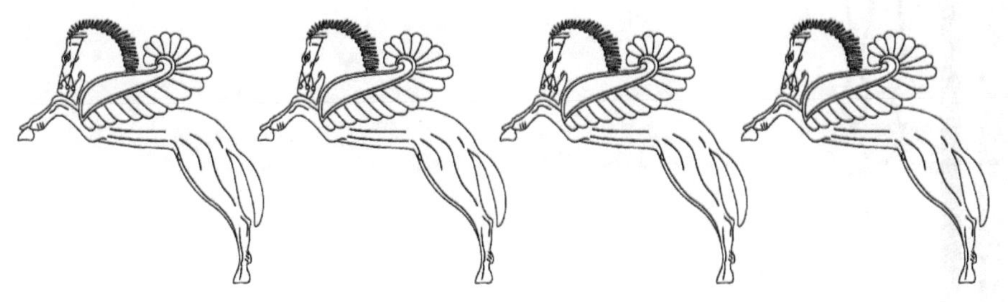

THE EPILOGUE

NOTWITHSTANDING THOSE post-season facts, or accolades, if you prefer to think of them in that way, it has been said, as the years have progressed, that most of the remaining "Boys" went back home, across the West Branch of the Susquehanna River, following the end of that undefeated and untied football season, not to mention their graduation thereafter, where they, eventually, disappeared into the pervading mist, which seemed to introduce each morning and salute each evening in the Appalachian Mountains, from whence they came. And subsequent thereto, they, and what they had legendarily done or been on a scholastic gridiron that season, became part of the folklore that made its way throughout those mountainous regions and, eventually, with endless discussion and disbelief, into mythology, years later, nearly everywhere in the State of Pennsylvania, if not in the Nation, itself.

With that in mind, I have been told, through the intervening years, that if you drive to the State of Pennsylvania and, thereafter, find your way across Interstate Route Eighty (80), which, virtually, bisects the State, east to west, on your way over toward Clinton County located near the center of the State. And if you, eventually, get off at an exit to a small, otherwise, inconsequential town, called Lock Haven, early in the fall of the year, when the sugar maple trees, endemic to the area, have turned the surrounding mountain sides into a brilliant red and orange hue, signaling to all of the nearby residents that it is the beginning of the football season there.

And if you, finally, stop at the corner of Fourth and Spring Streets in that town, where the J. Arlington Painter Football Stadium once stood, just below a no-longer-existing "Overhead Bridge." And if you remain standing there until the gray early evening sky has turned into an almost purplish-black, shortly before eight o'clock in the evening, when the games would have ordinarily begun. I have been told that you can actually hear at that point, "The Purple and White Marching Band" strike up "The Fight Song," once again, accompanied by the unmistakable voices of "The Seven Cheerleaders," singing it all over again.

And, moreover, if you listen, carefully, you can actually hear the words, although they may, initially, seem to be nothing more than the indistinct sound of a seasonal wind, beginning, as it usually does, at that time of the year and at that time of the evening, in the surrounding mountain sides, from whence they came, on its unmistakable way down into the valley, the Bald Eagle Valley. Traveling, thereafter, across the West Branch of the Susquehanna River, toward that inconsequential small town of Lock Haven, where they played, and where it all began, the legend, I mean!

What's more, I have been told that as "The Fight Song," and the accompanying voices of "The Seven Cheerleaders," begin to wane, until they have almost, indistinctly, become part of that seasonal wind, all over again, you can hear it now . . . "The Chant,"

I mean . . . by "The Seven Cheerleaders," occurring, as it usually does, at eight o'clock in the evening, precisely on the hour. And as soon as the chanting voices of those seven young ladies seem to tale-off into that darkening fall evening, so that they have become, indistinguishably, one and the same, there is an unmistakable rumbling up there, on that no-longer-existing "Overhead Bridge." It, of course, has been prompted by "The Chant," not unlike all of those years ago, when the legend became a reality and when eleven young men, outfitted in "The Purple and White" of the Lock Haven High School "Bobcats," became magical on a high school gridiron, and for all four quarters of a football game, too, against anyone, anywhere, at anytime.

Having said that, all of that, I have been told that if you look up, at that very moment, which is at eight o'clock in the evening, exactly on the hour, not a minute before or after, you can see them, all over again, just as they were before, in full uniform, no less, with cleats and helmets, too, rumbling along on that no-longer-existing, "Overhead Bridge:" David Wesley Maggs, John Albert Roller, Tomas Blaine Toner, Norris Jack Houser, David Ned Smith, Bill Delbert Karch and Jan Schwarz Bennett; or as they were known in the locker room, if not on the playing field, itself: "Wes," "Jack," "Tomcat," "Moose," "Smitty," "Midnight" and "Bender;" or, if you will, as they were journalistically known on the playing field that season, "The Seven Blocks of Granite."

And coming right behind them on that no-longer-existing, "Overhead Bridge," just as though they were on the "field of play," once again, are Charles Blaine Schiavo, William Francis Goodman, John Edward Englert, and David Lee Johnson; or as they were known in the locker room, if not on the playing field, itself, "Chub," "Bill," "Johnny" and, simply, "Dave;" or, as they were journalistically known on the playing field that season, "The Four Horsemen."

Of course, as a team, if you prefer to think of them in that way . . . the legendary way, I mean . . . they became known, on and off the playing field, at the time and for all time, as "The Boys From Across The River." See, in that regard, the column, entitled, "Lest We Forget," excerpted from the "Class Yearbook," known at the time as "The Gazette [of] Lock Haven High School [for] The Class of Nineteen Hundred [and] Fifty-Four," which has been made a part hereof and attached hereto, where the Class was reminded of, among a number of other notable things, "[T]he [B]oys [F]rom [A]cross [T]he [R]iver;" "The Big Snow and the Tyrone Game;" "The Lewistown Game" and "The Williamsport Game."

In the end, as those eleven young men begin to fade away, into the purplish black sky of another October evening in those Appalachian Mountains, while you're still standing there, as they have now during the seventy year interval since their legendary appearance on a high school gridiron, it is important to realize that they will never, actually, fade away. Not as long as another group of young men come together to face one another on a high school gridiron, in another game of football, early in the fall season, on another Friday evening, somewhere in the State of Pennsylvania, if not in the Nation, itself. Because those "Boys," who came out of the Appalachian Mountains and who crossed the West Branch of the Susquehanna River, in order to play a game of football for the traditionally beleaguered "Bobcats" of Lock Haven High School, and who finished their season undefeated and untied, sometimes in circumstances that were beyond belief, have become legendary for having done so, the subject of folklore thereafter, everywhere in that mountainous region, if not in the State, itself, and, seemingly, mythical, since that time, across this great Nation as one of the greatest assemblages of young men to ever play the game of football on a high school gridiron, if not the greatest of all time!

They were, quite simply, "The Legendary Boys From Across The River," who have become . . . following seventy years of discussion and disbelief in the folklore that has now found its way beyond that mountainous region, if not time itself . . . "The, mythical, Boys of '54."(1)

1). Below is a photograph of the team, the starting eleven, if you will, with the addition of Ken Miller and Wayne Englert, who, as part of the junior varsity, were regular substitutes at their positions that year. In order to include the latter player at his left guard position, Bill Karch, who normally started at that position, was moved into the backfield of the photograph, solely for the purposes of symmetry therein.

Second Row, Left to Right—Chub Schiavo, Ken Miller, Bill Goodman, Dave Johnson, John Englert, Bill Karch.
First Row—Wes Maggs, Jack Roller, Tom Toner, Jack Houser, Wayne Englert, Dave Smith, Jan Bennett.

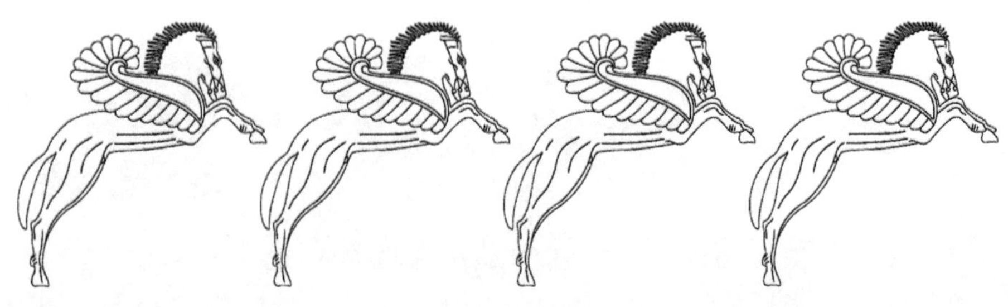

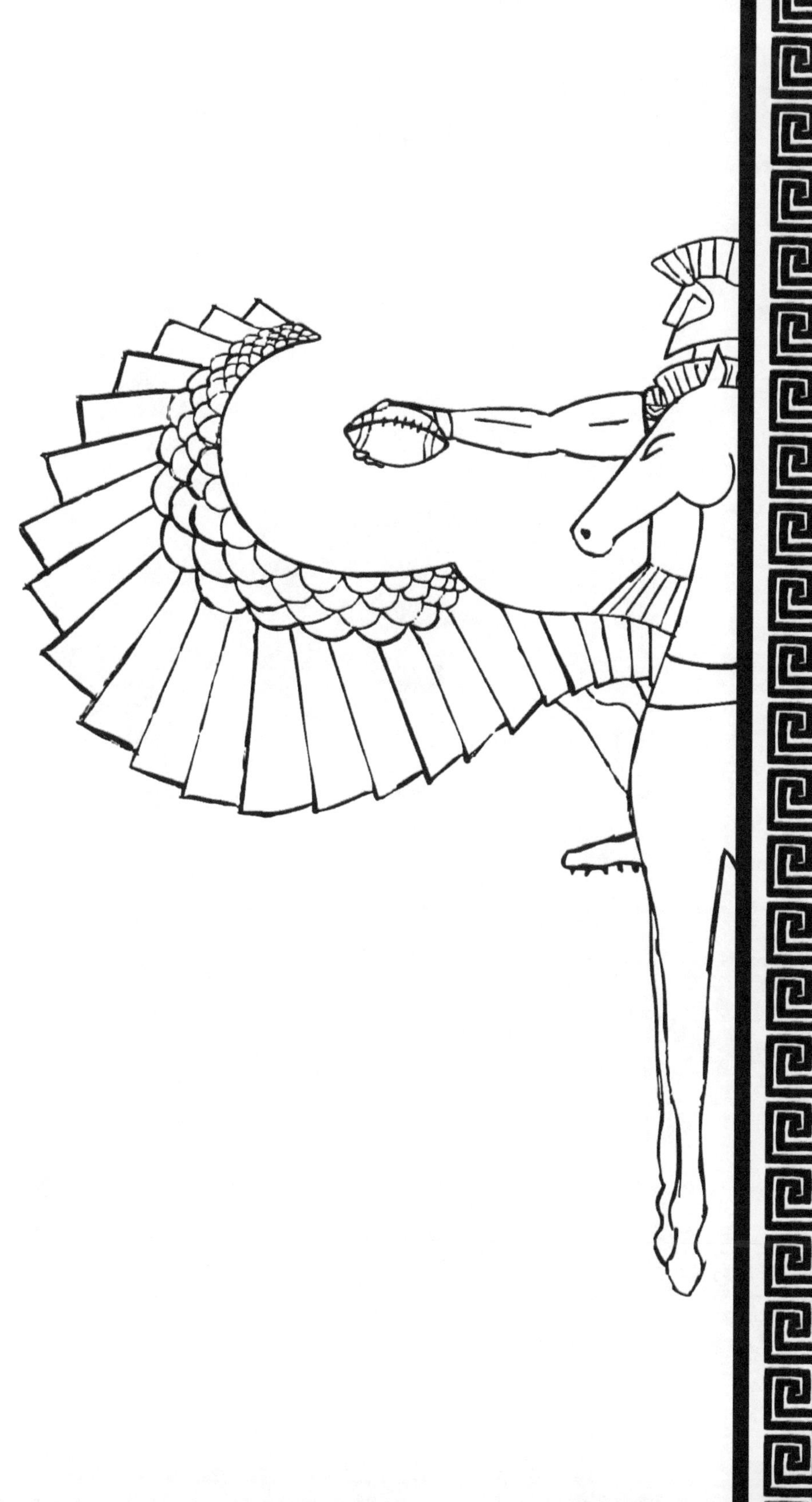

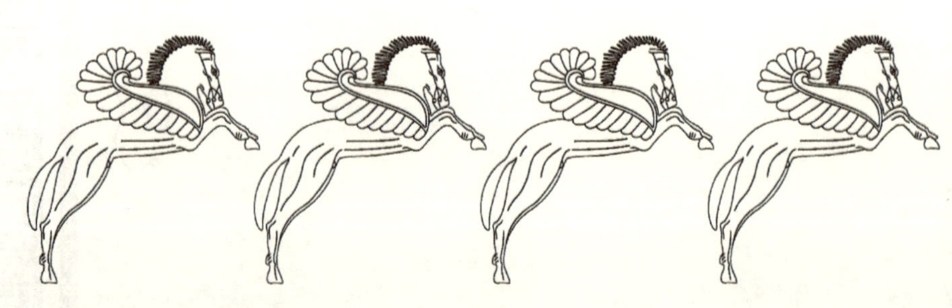

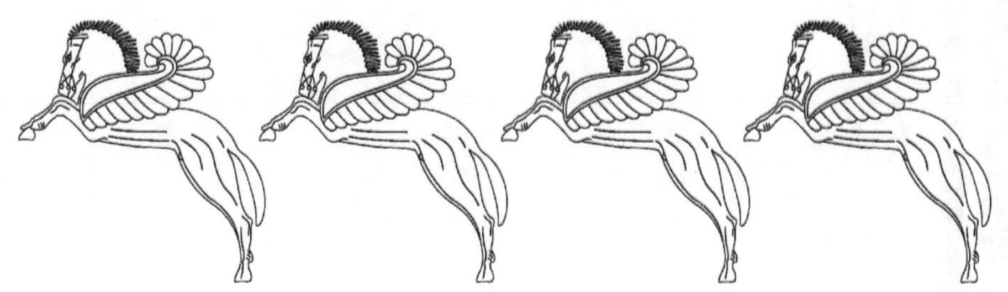

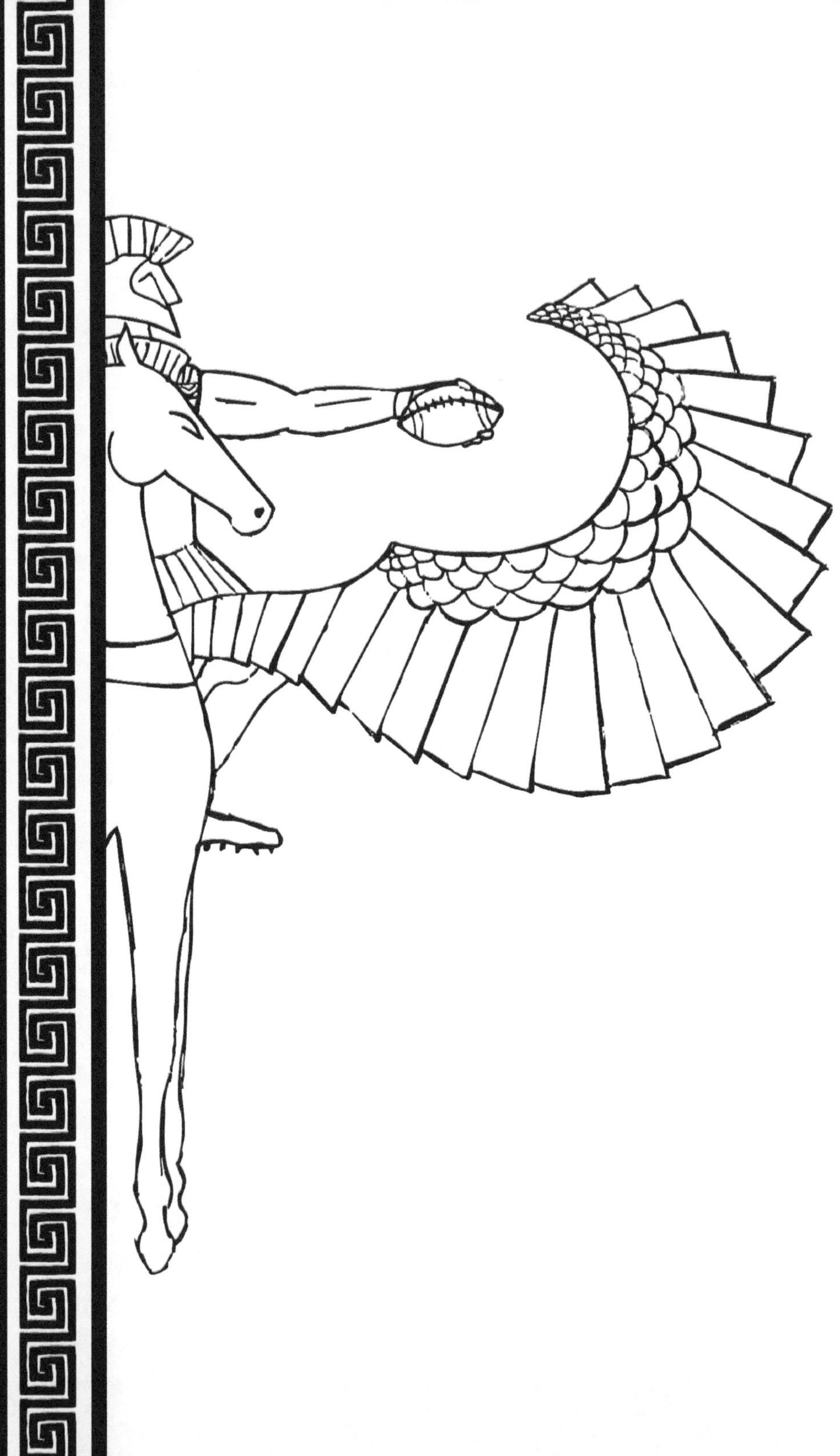

THE ATTACHMENTS

THE GAZETTE

LOCK HAVEN HIGH SCHOOL

THE CLASS OF NINETEEN HUNDRED FIFTY-FOUR

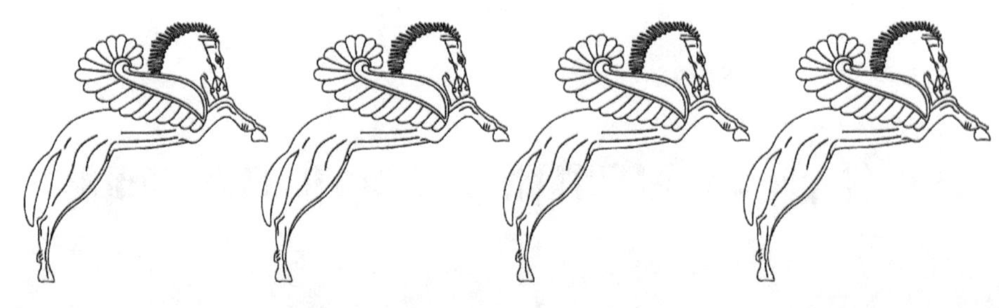

The Lock Haven High School Class of 1954
"The Class Of '54"

Lest We Forget . . .

The Big Snow and the Tyrone game.
The boys from across the river.
Mr. Hauke's plugged up keyhole in our Junior year.
Huck Derr's goatee.
True Talley and her Bowie knife at the lunch table.
Mr. Ferguson's last period Study Hall.
Joyce's week in the Chem Lab.
The day Jim Keller broke the desk in Mr. Cummings' room.
The Lewistown game.
Mr. Eisemann's third period Math Class.
Chapel on Fridays during football season.
The day Jack Houser found a padlock on his locker.
Jan Bennett's Llabesab.
Miss George's loops, ovals and rounds in Shorthand Class.
The hoagies we all loved at the football games.
Dragnet.
Mr. Hoch's lucky outfit and hair cut.
Junior-Senior Riots.
Miss Gresser's "All right, class. Let's get quiet."
When the cheerleaders and football team changed places in assembly.
The Williamsport game.
The Purple Whirl.

CLASS WILL

We, the class of 1954, bequeath the following:

Allen Joslyn's artistic talent to Jeff McCormick.
Nevin Greninger's brains to Jolene Grugan.
Barbara Dilling's musical ability to Eleanor Shamroy.
Rodney Reitz's crazy antics to Robert Cohen.
Louis Lantz's instrumental ability to Don Shiffler.
Jan Bennett's height to Ronald Askey.
Calvin Golumbic's skill in piano playing to Sonny Gallagher.
Paul Levi's ears to any head they will fit.
Dave Johnson's wrestling skill to Dick "Crow" Condo.
John Englert's athletic achievements to Bill Goodman.
Gilbert Collin's build to Curt Wetzel.
Janice Crissman's cheerleading ability to Barbara Anderson.
Ron Meyer's talent in photography to Donald Kochenour.
Chubby Schiavo's ability to stay out of trouble to Charlie Lair.
Jack Houser's blond hair to Sonya Renzo.
Robert Schadt's great singing ability to Ron Gardner.
All our wonderful ideas and achievements to Miss Dickey and the Junior GAZETTE Staff.

Our special thanks to the Faculty and Administration.

And to close, we, the entire Senior Class, leave our remaining class dues to Mr. Hauke to buy a lie detector.

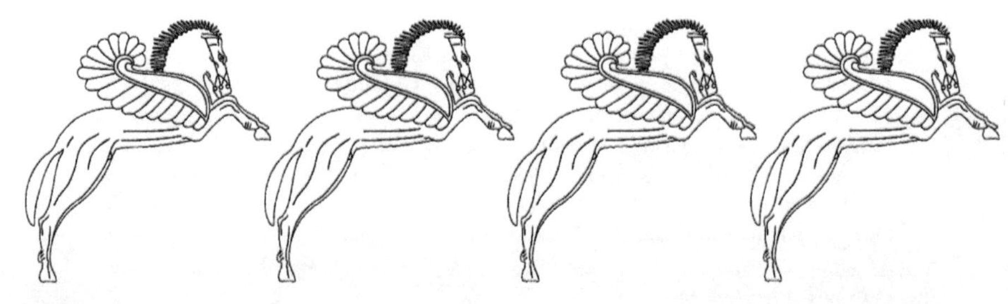

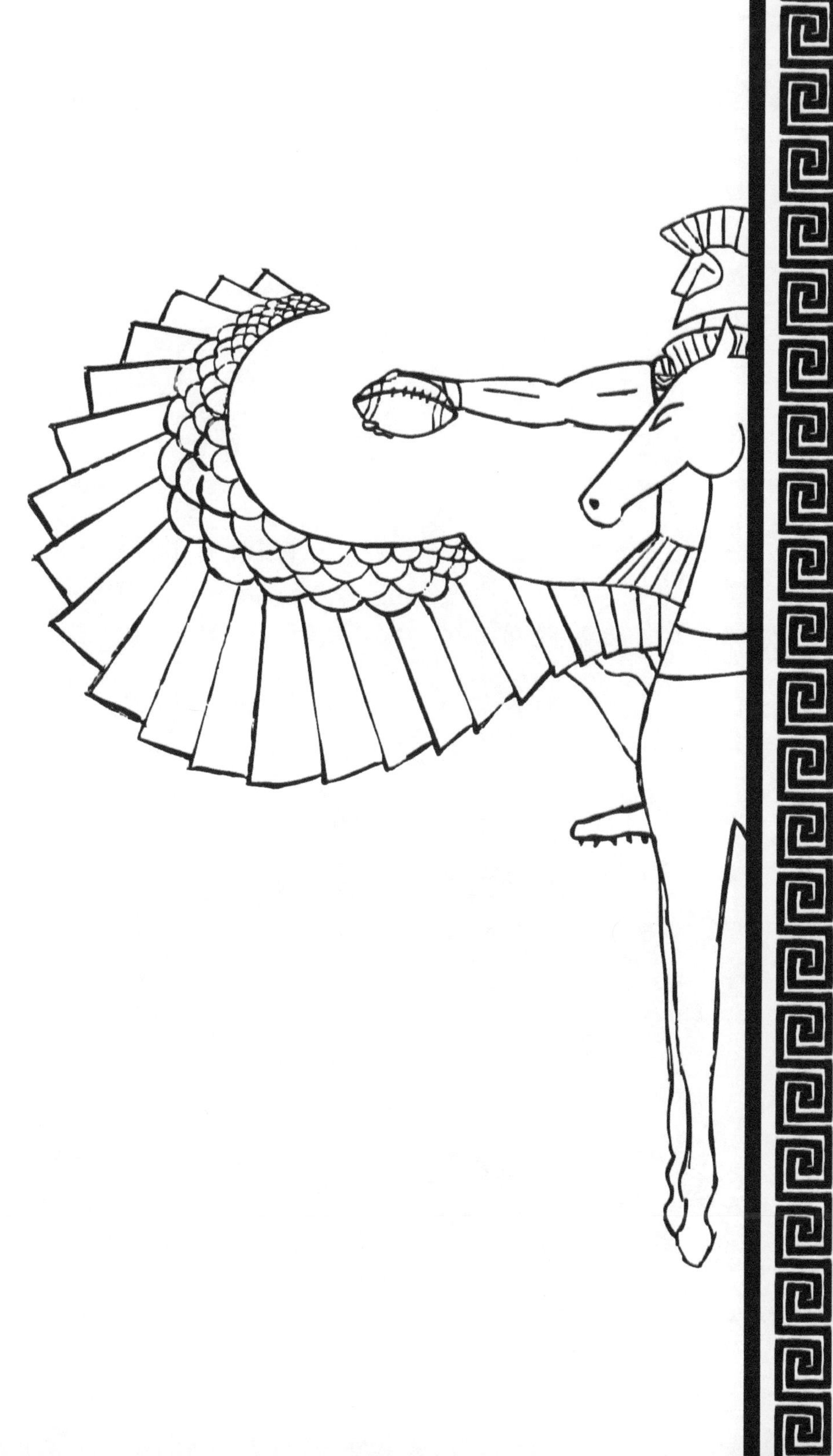

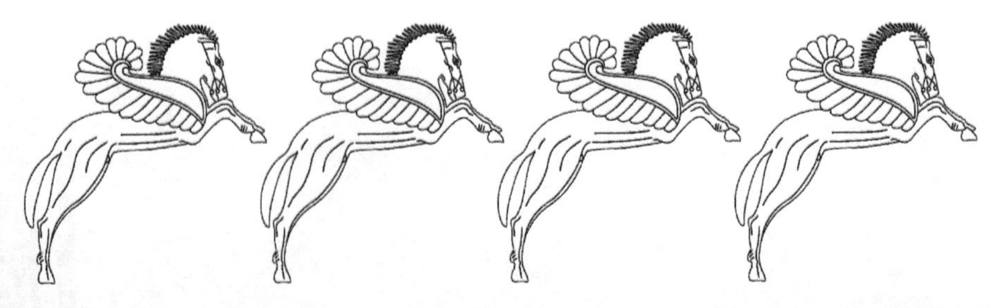

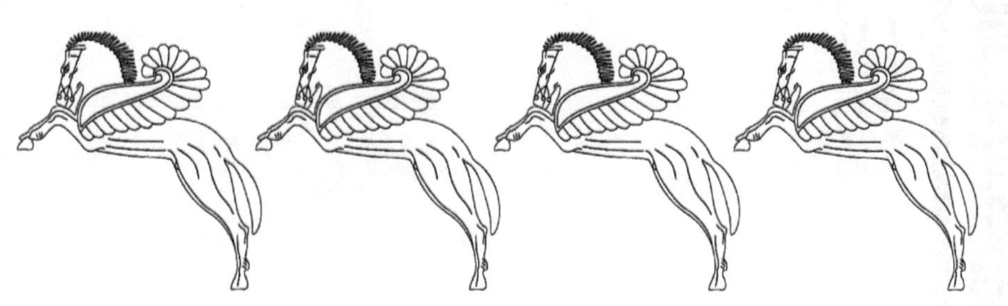

ABOUT THE AUTHOR

Cal Golumbic was an attorney for over thirty years, who retired as a partner from one of the largest law firms at the time in the Nation's Capitol. And for part of that time, he was also a Contributing Editor for the *Country Living Magazine*, writing a bimonthly column entitled, "Just A Country Boy." Upon his retirement from both positions, at nearly sixty years of age, he became a "Lecturer," for over ten years, in the English, Political Science and Philosophy Departments of the Liberal Arts College at Penn State University. Oh, yes, he also graduated from Lock Haven High School in 1954; "THE CLASS OF FIFTY-FOUR."

www.ingramcontent.com/pod-product-compliance
Lightning Source LLC
Chambersburg PA
CBHW020501310726
48979CB00016B/2747/J

* 9 7 9 8 2 1 8 7 1 9 8 0 7 *